I0768092

Their Lives

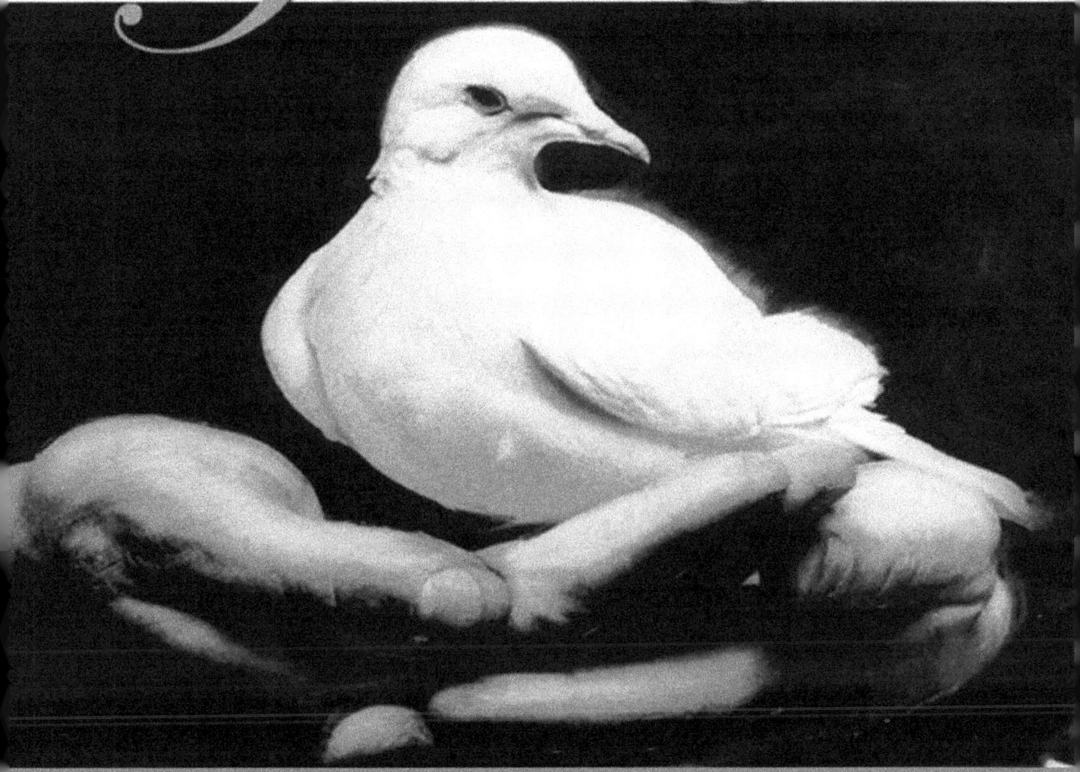

Were Unexpectedly Turned Around

a novel by **BETTY COOPER**

WORKBOOK PRESS LLC
187 E Warm Springs Rd,
Suite B285 Las Vegas NV 89119 USA

Website: https://workbookpress.com/
Hotline: 1-888-818-4856
Email: admin@workbookpress.com

Ordering Information:

Quantity sales. Special discounts are available on quantity purchases by corporations, associations, and others. For details, contact the publisher at the address above.

Library of Congress Control Number:

ISBN-13:   978-1-965732-68-7   Paperback Version
                978-1-965732-69-4   Digital Version

REV. DATE: 06/19/2025

Their Lives

WERE UNEXPECTEDLY TURNED AROUND

BETTY COOPER

THEIR LIVES WERE UNEXPECTEDLY TURNED AROUND

This story is about two powerful black families who lived in great luxury in the State of North Carolina. Mr. Ja'cob Jackson and his wife, Bella, had two sons. The oldest son's name was Ja'cob Jackson, Jr. and the youngest son's name was Antonio Jackson. Mr. and Mrs. Jackson built their own real estate agency in a wealthy suburb. Mr. Jackson also built his home close to his empire. He was a very proud man. He would always tell his family: "Be the best that you can be and live your best life and then something good will work in your favor."

Mrs. Bella Jackson worked hard right beside her husband. Her faith was secure in her trust in him, but her devotion was to her two sons. She encouraged them to do their very best in their schooling. Because of her motivation, both boys were A+ students. As a freshman in college, Ja'cob Jr. was studying to become a lawyer and he was at the top of his class.

Antonio was a senior in high school with a major in Communications. After school, Antonio would go to the YMCA where he would volunteer his services to help young boys and girls out with their homework. He became a big brother to some of the children who needed him. But Antonio really wanted to follow in his father's footsteps.

He told his father, "Dad, one day when I finish school, I want to go in the same field that you did and be successful just like you, Dad."

But his father turned and looked at him and replied, "Son, I don't want you to be just like me, I want you to be more than I could ever be." Mr. Jackson hugged his son and they began to laugh and talk to each other. After dinner, Mr. Jackson took Antonio aside to teach him how to run his business. Mrs. Jackson was in the kitchen cleaning.

The next day was a beautiful Saturday morning. The sun was shining so bright. The birds were singing in the trees next to Antonio's window and he could smell the scent from the kitchen where his mother was preparing breakfast. Antonio got up and took a shower. After he got dressed, he went downstairs to eat. When he sat down at the table, his parents took him by the hand and they prayed over the food. After everyone had eaten, Mr. Jackson asked Antonio what his plans were for today. He answered his father and said, "I will be here working in the yard today."

His dad said, "Okay son, I'm going to my office to finish closing on a house that I have just sold." Mrs. Jackson was cleaning the house and Ja'cob Jr. was away at school. As Antonio was walking outside, he noticed two moving vans going to the house across the street. Then he saw three cars pull up to their driveway. Antonio began cutting his grass, and then he noticed a beautiful girl about his age getting out of her car. By now, Antonio's mother had walked outside and approached him. He looked at his mother and said, "Mom, it looks like we have new neighbors."

She said, "I know, your father sold that house two weeks ago to the Smith family." Antonio kept working in his yard. His mother went back into the house. An hour later, Mrs. Jackson came back outside to where Antonio was working and she asked him to stop working for a minute and do her a favor. Antonio said, "What do you need, Mom?" "I need for you to clean yourself up. And then I want you to take a cake over to the Smith's home for me. I also want you to invite the Smith family over to dinner tonight."

Antonio put everything away and went inside to clean himself up. As he was walking away across the street, he noticed that this young lady was having trouble getting a box out of her car.

He walked over to her and said, "Hello, my name is Antonio Jackson." The young lady replied, "Hi, my name is Vicki Smith."

Then they stepped back and just looked at each other. Antonio began to think about how beautiful and breathtaking Vicki looked. She smiled at him, though she really didn't know what to say. When he smiled back, she asked him, "Would you like to come in and meet my parents?" And he said, "Yes… Oh, I forgot, my mom made you all a cake and she wants to know if you and your parents would come over to dinner tonight?" Vicki answered, "Let me ask my parents because we are so busy moving in. But if they can't come, I would love to come over."

Antonio began to smile even more at Vicki. "Vicki, you carry the cake and I will get the box out of the car."

By now, the movers had put everything into the house. As they were walking into Mr. and Mrs. Smith's home, Mrs. Smith stopped unpacking and said, "Well, who do we have here?!!" Vicki walked over to her mother and said, "Mom, this is Antonio Jackson from across the street." Antonio walked over to greet Mrs. Smith. She was happy to meet him. When Vicki called her father into the room, Mr. Smith said, "Hello, Antonio. My name is Charles Smith and I can see that you have already met my wife, Margaret, and my only daughter, the apple of my heart."

Antonio said, "Yes sir," then added, "Mr. and Mrs. Smith, my mother wanted me to ask if you would like to have dinner with us tonight?"

"Sorry son," Mr. Smith smiled, "we are unable to attend, but maybe Vicki can go."

"Well, it was nice meeting you. I will tell my mom that you will not be able to come over, she will understand."

As Antonio was leaving Vicki yelled out, "Wait for me, Antonio! I'll walk you out."

As they were walking outside, Antonio told Vicki that the suburbs had the most beautiful park and that it was on the next street over from their home. She looked at him and suggested, "Let's walk over there."

As they were walking, they began to tell each other about their lives. Vicki told Antonio that her father had a partnership with another company in the insurance business and that they are doing very well with it.

Antonio said, "Well, my father and my mother have their own organization in real estate, and when I go to college, I really want to work for them for a commission. There's lots of money in both my parents' companies and my brother and I are very blessed to have such a powerful background. It's not every day that you see a black family living out their dream, reaching the very height of their soul." By this time, there were some young ladies walking by that liked Antonio, but he just waved at them and kept talking to Vicki.

Vicki stopped him, "Antonio, what was that all about?"

Antonio answered, "Well, they were very attractive, but when I'm walking and talking to the most beautiful woman in the world, you have my full attention. Plus, those girls didn't show you any respect just now."

Vicki started laughing at Antonio, and then she said, "Who are you,

Antonio Jackson?" And he began to laugh. They both sat down and started asking each other questions.

Vicki asked Antonio if he had a girlfriend. And he said no. He said, "I try to keep my mind on my school work. Many of my friends date, but sometimes dating is just not for everyone."

"Antonio, you mean to tell me that you have not been with any girls before?"

"I'm not ashamed to say it, no, I have not! This is one of the subjects that I teach the young people. And if I'm going to teach it, then I must live what I say." Then he asked, "Vicki, how about you?"

She said, "I'm proud to say that no man has ever been with me. I'm still a virgin and no one is going to touch me but my husband."

That made Antonio's day. They stayed in the park and talked for a long time. As the evening was approaching, Antonio asked Vicki, "Are you still coming to dinner to meet my parents?" "I would not miss it for anything."

When she stood up, he reached for her hand and, as they were walking back toward their homes, Antonio invited Vicki to come to his church. She said yes.

Antonio walked Vicki to her door and then he ran across the street to his house. He came running into the house talking real fast to his mother and Mrs. Jackson said, "Slow down, son, I just can't understand a word that you're saying." She was so happy for him. But his father walked into the room, listened to him and commented, "Antonio, remember to always be a man and the things that I have taught you. If you do this, you will never go wrong, my son."

Antonio ran up the stairs to wash up for dinner. At seven o'clock that evening. Vicki walked over to his house and rang the doorbell. Antonio welcomed her in and she greeted his parents. After dinner, they all sat down to talk. Around nine o'clock, Vicki had to go back home. As she was getting ready to leave, Mrs. Jackson invited her to church the next morning. Vicki agreed. Mr. and Mrs. Jackson really liked Vicki. The next morning, everyone left very early because Mr. Jackson taught the adult classes at Sunday school and Antonio was involved in the youth program in church.

Vicki really enjoyed herself, and, after church, everyone went out to dinner.

Antonio and Vicki sat at the table together. After a long day, Antonio took Vicki home to prepare for school the next day. After he took Vicki home, he ran up to his room to see when the lights in her room were going to come on. He could see her room from his window. As he was sitting there, Antonio vowed to make Vicki his wife. Antonio was in a dream world all night thinking about Vicki. At one point, he could not even sleep. He just lay there, thinking about her. As Antonio was getting ready for school the next morning, he noticed that Vicki was not home; her car was gone. When Antonio arrived at school, he saw her car. As he was walking into the school, Vicki ran up to meet him. Antonio said, "Vicki, I'm surprised to see you here." Vicki replied, "I know, I had to leave out real early so I could get my assignment and find my classes."

"Let me see your assignment." As he was looking over it, he noticed that Vicki was in all of his classes and that she was an A student majoring in Computer Science and Math. As they were walking to their first class, all the students began to watch them because they had never seen Antonio so happy. Vicki looked at Antonio and said, "Antonio, you have an infectious smile and I like that about you."

After school was over, they both went straight home to do their homework. After they finished everything, Antonio and Vicki spent a lot of their time together and this routine went on for six months. By now, Antonio and Vicki had begun to date. Their parents sat both of them down and talked to them about the facts of life. Mrs. Smith said to Vicki, "We like Antonio a lot and he comes from a good family. One day he will make something good out of himself. But you are our daughter. We are so proud of you and we want the best for you. You are at the top of your class and we are going to send you to college to further your education." Mr. Smith added, "Baby, all we want you to do is just be careful. We just can't have anything getting in the way of your education."

Vicki responded, "Mom, Dad, I love you both with all my heart and I know that you want the best for me. I promise you that I will not let anyone or anything get in my way or stop my plans. I'm more responsible than that and you both have taught me very well. I do care for Antonio deeply and I may even love him, but I know how to stand. No one is going to touch me but my husband on my wedding night. So don't worry, Mom and Dad."

Mr. and Mrs. Smith were so happy to hear that. All they could do was just hug their daughter. But day after day, Antonio and Vicki spent every spare hour together. Vicki joined the choir under Antonio's direction and she also joined the YMCA with him and worked with children who had problems in school. Their parents were watching them closely. Antonio's dad finally went to him to have a man-to-man talk. But Antonio told his father that he had never had sex with anyone and that he and Vicki had talked it over and decided to wait for each other until the time was right. Mr. Jackson said, "Son, I'm so proud of you."

Two months later, everyone was making preparations for graduation. Both Antonio and Vicki were honor roll students. Antonio had an appointment at a great college and he wanted Vicki to ride with him. But she declined. She didn't think that would be good for either one of them. On the morning of graduation, Vicki's mother took her out shopping. Vicki and Antonio had to speak to their class that night due to the fact that they were at the head of their class. At the end of the graduation, people from college came onstage to present a four-year scholarship to Antonio Jackson. That really surprised Antonio. He realized that this scholarship would take him far away from home and from Vicki.

Then someone from another college made an announcement

and gave Vicki Smith a four-year scholarship. She was so happy that she began to cry. But it was a joyful cry. Antonio jumped up and down, he was so happy. That night after graduation, everyone wanted to go to the graduation party. But Antonio wanted to be alone with Vicki. He took her out to dinner and afterwards they walked in the park.

Antonio said, "Vicki, I need for you to sit down. I know we are going to be a long distance from each other, and that worries me."

Vicki looked at him and said, "Antonio, I have awaited all my life for someone like you. Let's get together once a month." He said, "That would be good." Then he kissed her. He began to feel as if he wanted to make love to her, but Vicki stopped him and said in a soft voice, "No one is going to get this but my husband." That's when Antonio dropped down on one knee and asked Vicki to marry him. Vicki said yes. Antonio and Vicki began to kiss each other.

Antonio held her and said, "We need to go and tell our parents." Vicki said, "Let's tell my parents first!" Antonio agreed.

As they began to walk away from the park, Antonio said, "Vicki, this is a dream come true for me."

"It is for me too."

When they arrived at Vicki's house, Mr. and Mrs. Smith were in the living room watching television. Antonio spoke up, "Mr. and Mrs. Smith, I have something to ask you."

Mr. Smith said, "You look nervous son, is everything okay?" "I'm feeling wonderful! What it is, is that I asked Vicki to marry me."

Mr. Smith sat up in his chair, looked at Antonio and Vicki and then said, "Son, don't you think that you are both too young for this? You both just finished school and are on your way to college. Don't you think that you need to wait until you finish college?"

Vicki said loudly, "No, Dad, we love each other and we want to be together!"

Mrs. Smith stood up and said, "Antonio, I love you like you were my own son and I feel it would be good if you and my daughter would wait until after you both finish college. And after that, if you two still want to get married, I would pay for it."

Vicki looked at her mother and said, "Thank you, Mom."

Mrs. Smith looked at her husband and said, "Baby, you are going to have to let Vicki fly her own wings one day."

Mr. Smith looked at his wife and daughter and asked them to leave the room. As they were leaving the room, Vicki walked over to her father and kissed him.

Mr. Smith walked over to Antonio and said, "I like you a lot and you come from a good strong background. I know that you love my daughter. And son, I'm glad that both of you love each other. All I want is my daughter happy, so I will lend her to you. Do your best to make sure that she is happy." He shook Antonio's hand and added, "Welcome to my family." Then Mr. Smith walked over to the window as he began to shed tears. He had his back to Antonio so he wouldn't see him cry. He said, "Antonio, it's not every day that you see black families staying in suburban neighborhoods." Then Mr. Smith said with a proud voice, "Look around, son, I didn't do so bad for myself." Then Mr. Smith just dropped his head. He couldn't say anything else.

Antonio looked at him and then he stood up and said, "Mr. Smith, Vicki and I will wait until we finish college, but we are going to spend each day calling each other." Mr. Smith said that was okay. Then Antonio said, "You

know that I love your daughter. Everything is going to be alright." Antonio began to walk towards the door then he looked back at Mr. Smith. "Sir, you have a good night."

Mr. Smith said, "Okay, son."

As Antonio was walking out the door, Vicki ran outside to him. She asked, "Is everything alright?"

Antonio said, "Yes. For now. My father is the one that I'm worried about."

Vicki said, "I will go with you." As they were walking across the street to Antonio's home, Vicki just held his hand. When they walked into the house, Mrs. Jackson was in the kitchen cooking. She heard the door open and went running over to Antonio and Vicki saying, "You both made me so proud. I loved those speeches that you both gave tonight."

Antonio said, "Mom, where's Dad?"

She said, "He's laying down. Is everything alright?" "Yes, Mom, I just need to talk to both of you."

Mrs. Jackson said, "Wait a minute, baby, let me get your father up." She went upstairs to wake up Mr. Jackson. He got up and went into the living room. Antonio announced said, "Mom, Dad, I have asked Vicki to marry me." Mr. Jackson asked Antonio, "Well, what did Vicki say?"

Antonio answered, "She said yes!!!"

His dad jumped up and said, "This calls for a drink!" Antonio said, "No, Dad, I don't drink."

Mr. Jackson said, "Son, you will tonight!"

By this time, Ja'cob Jr. had walked into the house. They had not seen Ja'cob Jr. for over a year. Mr. Jackson was so happy to see his oldest son that he didn't know just what to do. Mr. Jackson said, "Son, did you just go away and forget about us?" Ja'cob Jr. said, "No sir. I have really been in my studying." Ja'cob Jr. was hugging everyone. And then Antonio introduced him to Vicki.

Ja'cob said, "My goodness Antonio, did you go and get you a model? She is beautiful!"

Antonio replied, "I know, I just asked her to marry me."

Ja'cob took Antonio to the side and he asked him, "Did you lose your virginity? Did you get her pregnant?"

Antonio said, "No, man! We're both going to wait for each other. And how about you, Ja'cob?"

Ja'cob said, "I lost mine a long time ago."

Mrs. Jackson was so happy about Antonio and Vicki that she called her pastor and told him the good news. Pastor Tucker was so excited about it that he made a suggestion to give Antonio and Vicki a dinner and do something to honor them. Mrs. Jackson said, "Well, let's get together and we can make plans." After Mrs. Jackson got off the phone, she went over to Vicki and hugged her. By then, Antonio was getting ready to walk Vicki home. As they were getting ready, Vicki kissed Mrs. Jackson and called her "Mom." Mrs. Jackson loved that. Mrs. Jackson ran into the room where Mr. Jackson was laying down asleep. She was so happy. It wasn't long before she went off to sleep herself.

Vicki and Antonio were still outside talking, however. Vicki said to Antonio, "Baby, we had a long day, and right now, all I want to do is go   inside and have myself a long bath and then go to bed." But Antonio was still talking about making plans for their wedding. Antonio asked Vicki, "How do you feel about us? We made our big announcement today." Vicki said that it was wonderful as she was walking to her house. When she got to her door she turned to look at Antonio and said, "Goodnight baby, I love you." Antonio just smiled at her then ran across the street to his house.

When he went into the house, he noticed that everyone was already in bed. So he went in to take his shower and go to bed.

The next morning, everyone was up eating breakfast while Antonio was still asleep. Mrs. Jackson took his food up to his room and woke him up. He was still so happy that he didn't know what to say. Mrs. Jackson was doing all of the talking. By now, Ja'cob Jr. had walked into his room. He wanted Antonio to forget about marriage and just date around like him. Then the phone rang. It was one of his schoolmates, saying they were all getting together and going to the beach. Antonio told them that he needed to see what Vicki's plans were. He told his friends to let him call them back.

Ja'cob just looked at him and said, "You see, man, for the rest of your life, before you can make your own decisions, you are going to have to ask your wife. You are making a great big mistake."

Mrs. Jackson said, "Baby, don't listen to him. Vicki is a sweet girl and I like her. You know your heart." Antonio just lay there listening to everyone talk, but he didn't say anything. It wasn't long before Antonio asked everyone to leave his room. Mr. Jackson had already left for his office. Antonio called Vicki to tell her that the class was going to the beach. She said, "Call them back and tell them to wait for us." Antonio said, "Okay." Ja'cob Jr. overheard Antonio on the phone, walked back into the room and said, "Antonio, this is my first day back home to spend some time with you, Mom and Dad, and this is how you show your thanks to me? By going off with Vicki?!?" Antonio got mad at Ja'cob and began to yell at him, "Ja'cob, you don't even pick up the phone and call any of us. We haven't heard anything from you in one year!" By this time, their mother had run into the room to break them up. Ja'cob just walked out the door and then left the house. Antonio said, "Mom, I'm sorry about yelling in your house." She looked at him and said, "It's okay, son. You are going to be late. You get ready to go with Vicki and you all have fun. I will deal with your brother."

After Antonio picked up Vicki, Jac'ob walked back into the

house. His mother was saddened by the way he had acted and she let him know it, too. Ja'cob kept on saying. "Mom, I'm sorry." Then she wanted to know why he never called home. Ja'cob didn't have an answer for her, but he spent the rest of the day with his mom. They went out shopping and then they went to lunch. They just had the best of times.

Antonio and Vicki had met up with their friends. Everyone was playing together on the beach. Then they had a cookout. Everyone was so excited that they lost track of time as evening was drawing near. They decided to rent a room at a beautiful hotel. All the girls were supposed to stay on one floor of the hotel and the guys were supposed to have stayed on another, but everyone began to party. The guys brought alcohol and started getting intoxicated. Soon, everyone had coupled off and started having sex in their rooms.

Antonio and Vicki were still on the beach. Things began to heat up with them too. They were laying on their beach towel when Vicki kissed Antonio. He kissed her back. As they began to get deeper into the kiss, Vicki removed the top of her bathing suit. Antonio was going along with it until he remembered what their plans were. Antonio whispered into her ear and said, "Baby, no. I want you to give this to me on our wedding night because you are so very special to me." Vicki was speechless. But she calmed herself down. They got into the car and headed home. Vicki fell asleep on the long drive back.

By the time they arrived home it was three o'clock in the morning. Antonio walked Vicki to her door. Mrs. Smith was up and she opened the door. The first thing that she asked Vicki with a look of disapproval on her face was, "Did you sleep with Antonio tonight?"

Vicki walked past her mother and said, "No, Mom, I didn't sleep with him, but it wasn't because I didn't want to, it was because he stopped me." Mrs. Smith just smiled and went right up to bed. Vicki went up to her room and looked out her window, watching Antonio's house. She began to wonder if she had set her standards too high?

Antonio went into his house and found Ja'cob Jr. up watching television. Antonio went in there with him. He sat down beside Ja'cob. Ja'cob asked him, "Did you get it tonight, man?" Antonio asked, "Get what?"

Ja'cob said, "You know what I'm talking about." Antonio said, "No."

Ja'cob replied, "You have a real problem. You think that you are so much better than anyone else."

Antonio jumped up and said, "Because I want to give myself to my wife and her to me on our wedding night!? What's the matter with that?!?"

Ja'cob smirked said, "You just have to be like Dad." "What's your point, Ja'cob?"

Antonio shook his head then walked into his room and laid down. The yelling had awakened their mom and dad. But Mr. Jackson told his wife to let the boys handle it this time.

The next morning, everyone was getting ready for church. Antonio called Vicki to ask her if everything was alright. She said everything was fine and that she was getting ready for church too. Antonio suggested that they ride together and she agreed. It wasn't long before Vicki finished getting dressed and Antonio picked her up. The rest of the family met them at church.

When they arrived at church, everyone had already heard about their good news. As they were walking in, everyone stood up and congratulated them. Pastor Tucker asked Antonio and Vicki to sit up in the front. After the service was over, Pastor Tucker and the church family gave them a dinner. Everyone was so happy. At dinner, Pastor Tucker also recognized Ja'cob Jr. because he had just finished his first year of college and would to be home for his break. Mr. and Mrs. Smith were so proud of Vicki and Antonio. All Mr. and Mrs. Jackson could do was cry because they knew that their children would be going away for college.

It wasn't long before summer was over and they were on their way to college. It was so hard for Antonio and Vicki to leave each other. They had spent every day together. Antonio had to leave a week before Vicki did and he called her every day that week. When Vicki left home for college, Mr. and Mrs. Smith went with her to make sure she got settled into her new apartment. After the Smiths left, Vicki got homesick. She called her mother three times a day. And it wasn't long before Antonio called her. They promised each other that they would call each other every day. They also planned to meet each other once a month. Vicki had remained faithful to Antonio for those four years in college. Vicki was so good with her classes that she decided to take extra courses for more credits, and she also worked at the college office. Antonio had a full schedule as well. He really worked hard on his studies. It wasn't long before their four years of college were over and they were getting ready to graduate. Antonio got his bachelor's degree. He also graduated at the top of his class. Vicki's studies were focused on the executive branch of the government. After they both had graduated, they went back home to plan their wedding.

Everyone was rushing around, trying to get everything in order. Vicki wanted to have an outside wedding. Antonio and Vicki married on the first day of summer. The sun was shining, not a cloud in the sky. Everything was so beautiful. Antonio asked Ja'cob Jr. to be his best man. Vicki wanted her wedding to be in the park, because that's where they had spent a lot of their time together. Everything went according to plan. As Antonio and Ja'cob Jr. stood beside Pastor Tucker waiting to see Vicki, the band began to play the wedding song. Vicki stepped out from behind the curtain with her father, when Antonio saw her, he couldn't believe his eyes. Ja'cob Jr.'s mouth dropped open and he said, "Man, she is beautiful! She looks like a princess." All Antonio could do was cry. Pastor Tucker whispered in Antonio's ear, "Son, if you want to give her to me, that would be okay." Then Antonio smiled. Ja'cob said, "Just think, neither one of you have ever been with anyone, what a night you both are going to have." Antonio said, "You got that right."

The wedding was so big and beautiful that people were stopping beside the road, just taking pictures of it. All of their friends and loved ones were there. It was the happiest day of Antonio and Vicki's lives. After they said their vows, the first dances belonged to them. They danced to CeCe and BeBe Winans' song "It's O.K." They also danced off to Luther Vandross' song "Superstar/Until You Come Back To Me." Antonio and Vicki just had a beautiful wedding. Antonio just kept kissing his new wife. He couldn't keep his hands off his new bride. Ja'cob Jr. walked over to him and he said, "Antonio, do you need for me to tell you what to do?" Antonio shouted, "NO," and they both began to laugh. Soon, everyone was taking pictures with the bride and groom. As the wedding reception was coming close to an end, Antonio and Vicki began to open up their gifts. They thanked everyone for coming and for their gifts. Mr. and Mrs. Smith walked over to the table where Antonio and Vicki were sitting, and Mrs. Smith asked them to open their gift next. Vicki was so surprised to find two plane tickets and travel vouchers. One was for six days and five nights in Hawaii at a five-star hotel. The next trip was in Jamaica for six days and five nights. All expenses had been paid. Mrs. Smith also handed Vicki a small gift to open. It was a key to her new office as one of her father's secretaries. Antonio said thanks to everyone, but all Vicki could do was cry. Then Mr. and Mrs. Jackson walked over to their table and Antonio stood up and looked at his father. Mr. Jackson said, "Antonio, you have been a good son, never have I ever been to court or anything like that because of you. You are bright and you have a good head on your shoulders. You are going places. I'm proud of you, son. As a matter of fact, I'm proud of both of my sons."

"Get on with it, Ja'cob," Mrs. Jackson said. "Let him see what we have for him and his wife." Everyone started laughing. Mr. Jackson handed Antonio two gifts and Vicki one. Antonio opened his first present, a set of keys for his new office at his father's company. The second box had keys to their new four-bedroom house. Antonio jumped up and he just held onto his father and mother. Vicki also opened up her gift and she had a set of keys to their new home. Mr. and Mrs. Jackson welcomed Vicki into their family.

After Antonio had pulled himself together, he walked in the midst of everyone holding Vicki's hands. He said to everyone, "May I have your attention? Will everyone please lift your wine glasses in honor of my beautiful wife?" Then he turned to Vicki and said, "My beloved spake, and he said unto me, rise up, my love, my fair one, and come away. My beloved is mine, and I am hers. Thou hast ravished my heart."

Vicki smiled at Antonio and she responded to him. "Thy lips, O my spouse, drop as the honeycomb: honey and milk are under thy tongue; and the smell of thy garments is like the smell of Leb'a-non."

"I sleep, but my heart waketh: it is the voice of my beloved that knocketh, saying open to me, my sister, my love, my dove, my undefiled: for my head is filled with dew, and my locks with the drops of the night."

"My beloved put in his hand by the hole of the door, and my bowels were moved for him."

"I rose up to open to my beloved; and my hands are dropped

with myrrh, and my fingers with sweet smelling myrrh, upon the handles of the lock."

Antonio turned to the crowd and said, "We have just spoken from Song of Solomon." And then Antonio embraced Vicki and kissed her. The people were standing in amazement of what they had just heard. Antonio and Vicki each took a drink and then left the wedding party. They were headed to the airport to board their plane to Hawaii.

While they were on the plane, Antonio asked Vicki, "Did your mother design the whole wedding?"

Vicki started laughing and said, "Yes, my mother used to be a home designer before she started helping my dad." Antonio said, "Well, she did an excellent job."

Vicki said, "I know."

They both were excited when they arrived at their hotel in Hawaii, and the men in the lobby took care of their baggage while they checked in. The clerk at the desk gave them the keys to their suite. When they got to the suite, Antonio picked Vicki up and carried her into the room. Once inside the room, they saw that the hotel administrator had placed gifts and a fruit basket along with more gifts from their family there. Antonio and Vicki's dream had come true because they loved each other. Vicki went into the bathroom to take a shower and Antonio joined her. After their shower, Antonio pulled back the bedspread and waited patiently for his bride. As Vicki walked into the room, she had on this sexy red lace gown. When

Antonio saw her, he began to get so nervous. But Vicki was ready to receive him unto herself. As she began to kiss him very passionately, she asked him, "Do you want to have children right away or do you want to wait?"

He said, "Let's start right away."

Their sexual desire was so hot. In that very moment, Antonio went somewhere he had never dreamed of. Vicki was so overwhelmed that when it was over, she couldn't say a word. After making love to his wife, Antonio whispered into Vicki's ear and he said, "Is it all that you hoped for?"

She answered, "Yes, and more than I ever hoped for."

This was the first time that either of them made love. As Antonio was holding his wife in his arms, Vicki fell asleep. Antonio couldn't believe that he did it. He was so excited, he just laid back and rested. They fell asleep for hours.

At about 10:00 p.m., they got up and went to a late show, and they ate out. They didn't get back to their suite until 2:00 a.m. The next morning, Antonio made love to his wife again. After all the good times that they had, the days went by fast, and it was soon time for them to leave for their trip to Jamaica. As they were leaving Hawaii, Vicki began to take pictures of everything she saw. When they were traveling to Jamaica, Vicki stopped to call her parents, just to check up on them. Antonio called his parents also.

They were having the best of times, and soon they arrived in Jamaica. The people treated them like a king and princess. On the first night, Antonio wildly made love to Vicki. They taught each other and they spent every day doing what their heart desired. As their time was coming down to the end, Vicki and Antonio danced the night away. They discovered each other. The next day, they were making preparations to go back home. Antonio looked at Vicki and he said, "Baby, you have enriched me in ways that I can't explain."

Vicki said, "We are walking into excellence." Antonio just smiled and held onto Vicki's hands.

After they arrived at their new home, they couldn't believe their eyes. While they were away on their honeymoon, Mrs. Jackson and

Mrs. Smith had placed new furniture all through the house. It looked so beautiful. Vicki got ready to call her mother, but Antonio said to her, "Wait, I have need of you right now." He picked Vicki up and carried her into the bedroom then made love to her. Two hours later, Mrs. Smith was passing by and saw that they were both home, so she stopped in to say hello. She found them undressed. Vicki yelled out, "Mom, what are you doing here?"

Mrs. Smith said, "Well, baby, I was passing by and saw that you both were home so I just let myself in." Vicki said, "Have you ever heard of knocking, Mom?"

Mrs. Smith said, "Vicki, I'm so sorry." Mrs. Smith was so happy to see her daughter, though. As she was leaving, Vicki said, "Go home, Mom."

Antonio was covering himself up. He didn't know what to say.

Later on that evening, Mrs. Smith and her husband were so happy that they gave a cookout at their house. Mrs. Jackson came over to help cook.

Everyone was there but Antonio and Vicki. While waiting for the newlyweds, Mrs. Smith began to tell Mrs. Jackson how she had walked in on Antonio and Vicki. Mrs. Smith said, "Oh yes, they would already be here if my daughter would just let him up for some air." They began to laugh, and by then some of the neighbors began to come over. Meanwhile, Antonio and Vicki were still at home getting dressed. After they got dressed, Antonio said, "Vicki, it is such a beautiful day, why don't we walk to the cookout? It's just over the next street."

Vicki responded, "Okay."

As they were walking hand in hand, Antonio cut across the park. He began to talk about the first time he saw Vicki.

"Vicki, we were no more than seventeen years old when we finished school."

Vicki said, "That's because we did a lot of studying and our parents started working with us at a very early age."

Antonio continued, "Now that we are twenty-one years old, I just don't want to wait a long time to have my own children." "Well, Antonio, the way we are going at it, your dream may be coming true very soon."

And then he asked, "Vicki, how do you feel about it?"

"Well, I wanted to do more things, but if this is so important to my loving, handsome husband, then this is what I want too." By this time, they had arrived at Mr. and Mrs. Smith's home. When they walked up, they heard the music playing and they saw a lot of people. Mrs. Jackson walked over to them and said, "Children, why didn't you let anyone know that you were home?"

Mrs. Smith said, "Oh, I could answer that." Antonio and Vicki just started laughing. Vicki then walked over to her mom and said, "Mom, I thought that you were having a cookout, but you look like you're having a party."

Mrs. Smith said, "Well, baby, your dad just got a break from his work and he wanted to give everyone something for working so hard for him."

Vicki said, "Is Dad giving bonuses today?" Mrs. Smith said, "Yes."

But Vicki noticed one young lady watching Antonio. All the men were sitting around the table talking. Vicki wasn't worried about Antonio, because she knew that he was honorable and faithful to her. Finally, the young lady approached Antonio, not knowing that this was her boss's daughter's husband. As she walked over to him, Antonio spoke to her and was real nice, all the while looking at Vicki and smiling. Vicki was used to women coming on to Antonio. Antonio said, "Let me introduce you to my wife." But the young lady wasn't willing to meet Vicki and just walked away. Mr. Smith saw what happened, but as he was approaching the young lady. Vicki said, "No, Dad, we can handle it."

Mr. Smith said, "No, baby, this is my house and I am her boss."

Vicki said, "But if you get on her, it will look like I don't trust my husband. Please, Dad, just leave it alone, because I know where Antonio's heart lies: with me."

Mr. Smith went back to the table where the men were talking, but he kept his eyes on the young lady. Everyone began to have a good time, and it wasn't long before the cookout was over. As everyone was leaving, Ja'cob Jr. arrived. He wanted to talk to Antonio before he left for New York City. Ja'cob Jr. had a law office. While they were talking, Vicki was helping her mother and Mrs. Jackson clean up. Mr. Smith had gone inside to get ready for bed. The cookout lasted until 10:00 p.m. Antonio and Vicki said their goodnights to everyone and then they began to walk home.

Vicki asked Antonio, "Did you have a good time?"

Antonio looked up at the sky and said, "Baby, we have a full moon tonight and the stars are shining so bright."

Vicki started to laugh. She said, "Antonio, no one asked you about the moon and the stars." They both laughed. Antonio picked Vicki up and carried her on his back. As they were walking into their home, Antonio said, "Baby, you have nothing to worry about, because I only have eyes for you. You are my whole world, and I have waited far too long for you to mess up now."

They went into their bedroom to get ready for the night. Vicki went into the bathroom to take her shower. Antonio started to read a good book. As Antonio was sitting down reading, Vicki walked out of the bathroom, sat down on their bed, looked at Antonio, and said, "Baby, generally, I'm not an insecure person, but I do get jealous when beautiful women are throwing themselves at my husband. Now that we are married, I guess, in some ways, I have become jealous." Antonio just looked at Vicki as she was talking. He put the book down and walked over to where she was sitting. He said, "Vicki, I understand, because I really feel the same way that you do. If I ever saw a man trying to come on to you, I would be jealous too. But the one thing I hold dear to my heart is that I know I can trust you and you can trust me. You are my earth angel. And I have a solution, the next time a woman comes anywhere near me, I will run as fast as I can into your arms for help."

They both began to laugh. After they finished laughing, Antonio looked at Vicki and said, "Baby I need to talk to you about something very important."

Vicki responded, "What is it?"

"Well, Vicki, we are twenty-one years old now, and we are married. All of our lives, our parents have taken care of us. They paid for our wedding, they bought us this house, and now that we are married, it's time for me, as your husband, to take care of my wife and stop depending on our mothers and fathers. Tomorrow I will be starting my new job with my dad. I already know what to do because my dad used to take me to work with him, plus I took Real Estate in college. I have my own master plan for what I want to do."

Vicki replied in a soft tone, "Antonio, all of my life, my parents have given me everything that I ever wanted. If they offered me something and I didn't take it, they would think I'm going crazy."

Antonio said, "Vicki, you will be just fine. Look around you, you have everything."

"Not everything, Antonio."

Antonio smiled at Vicki and said, "Please, baby, just meet me halfway?" Vicki didn't say anything, she just pulled back the covering and laid down. Antonio went into the bathroom to take his shower. When he returned, he found Vicki asleep. Early the next morning, Antonio was getting ready to go to work and Vicki was still asleep so he did not wake her. He just wrote her an "I love you" note then left it on the nightstand beside the bed. Vicki

was awakened by the phone ringing. It was her mother. She wanted Vicki to go shopping with her. Vicki agreed to go. After Vicki got ready, her mother picked her up. Vicki had the best of times shopping with her mother. She had such a good time, in fact, that she forgot her cell phone. Antonio was trying to reach her all day, but was unsuccessful, so he left his job early to go home to check on Vicki.

When he arrived home, he saw that her car was in the driveway and he went running into the house but did not see her, so he called Vicki's father's home. When Mr. Smith answered the phone, Antonio asked him, "Have you seen Vicki today?"

He said, "Yes, she's out shopping with her mother."

Antonio expressed his relief and then they began to talk about something else. When Vicki and her mother finished shopping they went back to Vicki's home to put up some more designs. When she got there, Vicki saw Antonio's car, and she remembered what she and Antonio had talked about. As she and her mother were about to reach the door, Antonio opened it and helped them with their bags and never brought the subject up. He just

kissed his wife. He was so glad to see her. Antonio knew Vicki was spoiled, so he just let her have her way. While Vicki and her mother were fixing up the house, Antonio started dinner. After he finished cooking, he made them both a plate. All he wanted for Vicki was happiness. After everyone ate, Mrs. Smith left and went home.

Antonio watched TV until it was time to go to bed. Throughout the rest of the week, Vicki really fixed up the house, making it look just like she wanted. Antonio worked real hard. Mr. Jackson was paying Antonio by the clock, and when he saw how good Antonio was, he started paying him a commission of six percent with every house that he sold. Antonio was very happy about that even though he hadn't been on the job more than two weeks. Vicki had not started to work yet. The following Monday, Vicki went to work at her father's company. When she arrived, she went straight into her father's office. Mr. Smith showed her around and took her to her new office, where he gave Vicki her assignment for that day.

While Vicki was working at her desk, the young lady that was at her parents' house, walked into her office and said, "Well, well, isn't this the boss's daughter? And you have your very own office, it must be nice."

Vicki just looked at her and said, "You have a lot of nerve coming into my office with this attitude." Then she asked the young lady, "What is your name?"

The young lady answered, "It's Nancy White."

"Nancy, the next time that you come into my office without knocking, or you show this attitude up with me, I will have your job."

As Nancy was walking out of Vicki's office, one of the head secretaries overheard what Vicki was saying and took Nancy to Mr. Smith's office and reported her. Mr. Smith looked at Nancy sharply and told her, "I know that this cannot be true, because if you are making things uncomfortable for my daughter then you need to clear your desk now."

After Mr. Smith had his little talk with Nancy, she went back to Vicki to apologize. In the weeks that followed, everything worked out well with Nancy and Vicki.

After working on the job for one month, however, Vicki became sick. She could barely eat, and early one morning, she was throwing up. Antonio thought that the job was getting to be too much for her. Vicki had been sleeping a lot on her days off.

Antonio called her mother and Mrs. Smith came right over to see what was wrong. After Mrs. Smith arrived, she helped Vicki dress and they took her to the doctor. After the doctor checked Vicki, he told her that he was sending her blood work to the lab. Mrs. Smith was smiling because she knew what that meant. But Antonio and Vicki were going all to pieces. They were so worried that they didn't know what to do.

When the doctor came back into the room he said, "Congratulations, Mr. and Mrs. Jackson, you are getting ready to have a baby. Mrs. Jackson, you are six weeks pregnant." Mrs. Smith fell back into the chair and said, "Thank God, my very first grandbaby." Antonio just held Vicki and cried like a baby, he was so happy. Then he also rushed to the phone to call his mother and father to tell them the good news. After Antonio told his parents, Mrs. Jackson wanted to speak to Vicki, but Antonio said that they could see Vicki when he got her home. Mrs. Jackson called Ja'cob Jr. in New York to tell him the good news. Everyone was so excited.

They were calling all the family members and even their friends. Mrs. Smith called her husband at his job. After Mr. Smith heard the good news, he just closed the door to his office and cried because he didn't know what to say.

After Antonio got Vicki home, he helped her up to the bedroom to lay down. The whole family waited on Vicki for the remaining seven and a half months. At the end of her pregnancy, Vicki went into labor and stayed in labor for four hard hours. Antonio was right there beside her along with Mrs. Smith and Mrs. Jackson. Mr. Smith and Mr. Jackson stayed in the hallway because they couldn't stand to hear her cry. In that fourth hour of labor, Vicki pushed a seven-pound boy into the world. She named him Antonio Jackson, Jr. after his father. Antonio was so proud of his new baby

boy. After two days, the doctor sent Vicki home with her new baby. Antonio took off from his job for two weeks to be with them. Their parents were there around the clock as well. Vicki didn't have a need for anything.

Antonio went to Vicki while she was feeding the baby and said, "Vicki, I don't want you to go back to work."

Vicki said, "I know, I was thinking the same thing because I could never leave my baby. I have to be here for him."

After Antonio Jr. turned six months, Vicki went to her husband and she asked him, "Antonio, have you ever thought about starting your own company?"

"Yes, but I need to talk to my father to let him know what I'm going to do." "Then why don't you go over to his home now and talk to him?"

"I don't think that Dad is going to like this."

"Well, you'll never know what he thinks if you don't get over there and talk to him."

As Antonio was walking out the door, he kissed Vicki and his son. Antonio decided to walk through the park and think about what he was going to say to his father. After Antonio arrived at his father's home, Mr. Jackson met him at the door.

He said, "Antonio, how is my grandbaby?"

Antonio said, "Dad, he is growing so fast." And then he said, "I need to talk to you. Now that I have a wife and a new baby, I have a big obligation to them."

Mr. Jackson said, "Well, son, let it out, tell me what you want me to know."

Antonio looked at his father and he said, "Well, Dad, I'm thinking about leaving your company and branching off on my own."

Mr. Jackson said, "What, son? How long have you been thinking about this?"

"For some time now."

"How did you come up with something like this? Son, how would you make it? You have my only grandbaby."

"Dad, I'm starting my own company."

"Well, son, I see that your mind is made up. I'll give you two months and if things don't work out for you, then you can have your job back."

Antonio agreed to that. After they finished talking, Antonio walked back home. He went back to Vicki and told her what he said.

Vicki said, "Baby, I was checking the Internet and I saw that there are going to be a lot of brokers coming into town tomorrow. It would be nice if we could go to these meetings."

Antonio said, "Well, call your mother and see if she would watch our son so we can go to the meeting." Vicki called her mother and Mrs. Smith said it would be an honor to watch her only grandson. The next day, everything was going so well. They went to the meeting and met a lot of important people. It wasn't long before Antonio started his own business. Antonio

was doing great, he climbed to the top of his success, and it wasn't long before Antonio was selling million dollar homes. After Antonio Jr. turned two years old, Vicki was pregnant with her second child. It wasn't long before Vicki had another little boy. He weighted eight pounds and Vicki and Antonio named him Ja'cob Jackson III after his father and brother. Antonio was overjoyed. The whole family supported them.

Mr. Jackson went to his son and said, "Antonio, you have made me so proud." Everyone began to spend a lot of time at their house. Antonio and Vicki did not complain because they knew that their boys were the only grandchildren on both sides of the family. They welcomed the help with the boys. After Ja'cob was born, Vicki began to write children's books for her boys and, since she was a gifted painter, she began to paint pictures of the boys. She was teaching Antonio Jr. how to read. Vicki made sure that everything was done well at home.

As the boys grew older, Vicki began to get somewhat restless. Antonio noticed that Vicki was not like herself, so he brought her gifts and roses. Antonio did everything to make Vicki happy. Then one night after dinner, Vicki went to Antonio and said, "Baby, we need to talk."

He looked into her eyes and said softly, "What's the matter, baby?" She answered, "You know that I love you deeply and I love our boys. Antonio, we have the best life, but something is missing, I need more."

"Baby, what is it that I could do to help?"

"I don't know. I really don't know what it is."

"Have you ever tried to talk to your mother about what you don't know right now?" Vicki began to smile and she said, "No!!"

"Why don't you call your mom tomorrow and invite her out to breakfast and you both do a little shopping. You should talk to her about the way you feel because you both are so close. I love you, Vicki."

Vicki just looked at Antonio and put her arms around him. For a long while, she just held him.

The next morning, Vicki got up and she got the boys dressed to go over to Mrs. Jackson's house. Then she called her mother to invite her out for breakfast. After making arrangements with her mother, she called Mrs.

Jackson to tell her that the boys were dressed and ready for her to pick them up. Mrs. Jackson said, "Okay. I'll be over to get them in five minutes." It wasn't long before Mrs. Jackson arrived, and when the boys saw her, they ran to their grandmother. Mrs. Jackson noticed that Vicki was distanced and her speech was very short.

Mrs. Jackson walked over to hug her and, as she was hugging her, Mrs. Jackson said, "Vicki, what's wrong? I notice that you have something on your mind. Is there anything that I can do?"

Vicki said, "No, I just really need some time to myself."

Mrs. Jackson said, "Well, baby, we're going to get ready to go."

The boys kissed Vicki before they left. When Mrs. Jackson was about to leave, she turned to Vicki and said, "Vicki, you know that we all love you and you can talk to me about anything." Vicki said, "Thank you."

While Vicki was getting ready to leave, Antonio called her and said, "Vicki, I love you with my whole heart, you are the air that I breathe, you are my whole world. If something is wrong or your heart is broken or hurting in

any way, my life is not complete." Vicki thanked him for saying that.

After Vicki finished talking to Antonio, she got dressed to meet her mother. She met her mom at Cooper's restaurant.

Her mother was already there when she arrived. Vicki said,

"Hi Mom, how long have you been here?" "I just arrived."

"Mom, have you already ordered?"

"Yes, I have ordered for both of us. Our food will be ready soon." "Mom, let me ask you something. Do you think that I am being selfish?"

Mrs. Smith looked at Vicki and she said, "First of all, you need to tell me how you are feeling."

"I don't know how to explain myself, all I know is something is missing in my life."

"Oh baby, you have finished college, you have a beautiful home, and a wonderful husband and two beautiful boys. But you are just like your mother, there's nothing wrong with wanting more. We are wealthy people and we worked hard for it. Vicki, you have everything going for you. You have a major in so many subjects.

Why don't you talk it over with Antonio about your going back to work? Vicki, you are good with telling children's stories and you have written some children's books. Why don't you go on the Internet to see if you could get an agent to read your books?"

"Mom, I have never thought about that! This is a good idea. Thanks, Mom."

"Oh baby, that's what Mom is for." By this time, the waitress had brought their food to the table. Vicki was happy now. As they were eating, Vicki suggested that she wanted to take her mother out shopping. Mrs. Smith began to laugh and said, "Here's my baby that I know."

After paying for their food, they both began to walk from shop to shop. After they finished shopping, Vicki went home to prepare Antonio and the boys' dinner. She cooked their favorite food. She was so happy. When Antonio got home, he smelled all that good food cooking. He walked into the kitchen and saw Vicki was cooking and singing, – what a surprise for him! When she looked and saw Antonio, she just ran and jumped into his arms. Vicki told Antonio the good news.

As Vicki was talking, Antonio sat down and just listened to her. When she finished talking, Antonio really didn't understand her fully, but he said, "Baby, all I want is to see you happy, and if this makes you happy, I will stand beside you and will support you all the way. Now, can you please tell me when my boys are coming home? And when are you going to finish cooking?" Vicki said, "Everything is ready, so let me call your mother and tell her to bring our boys home while you wash up for dinner."

For weeks, Vicki worked on her books and went on the Internet looking for agents. After six months, a well-known agent from California e-mailed Vicki about her children's books. She wanted Vicki to e-mail them information. And when Vicki did, she just loved her books. This agent wanted Vicki to fly out to California. But Vicki told her that she needed to talk everything over with her husband. The agent agreed. That evening when Antonio got home from his office, Vicki ran up to him with excitement all over her face. Vicki was talking so fast that Antonio could not understand her, so he said, "Vicki, slow down."

Vicki said, "I don't have time to slow down, I'm leaving for California in the morning."

Antonio said, "What?!!"

"Baby, you are not listening to me. I have a big agent and she wants to meet with me tomorrow in California at 12 noon. I have got to pack!"

"Honey, how long are you going to be gone?" "Just three days, I will be back home soon."

"Baby, I'm happy for you, but this is kind of short notice. If you could just wait until the end of the week then we could both fly out there."

Vicki looked at Antonio sharply then she walked in front of him and said, "What?! Antonio, are you not understanding me? I'm leaving in the morning, early." Antonio just stood his ground and said, "Vicki, I know that you worked hard on your books and you have earned everything that you have, but I just don't want you to rush into anything."

Vicki began to talk loudly to Antonio, saying, "Antonio, you have forgotten that I majored in business. I'm not rushing into anything, I just know a good deal when I hear one."

Antonio yelled, "Vicki, what about the boys and me? We need you here!"

Vicki shouted, "Is this all I'm good for, being your sex partner or cleaning up after the boys? Oh!! Being your maid?"

Antonio couldn't say anything, he just rushed past her, and he walked real fast outside. Vicki ran to the window crying, looking at Antonio. Then she rushed over to the phone and called her mother. Vicki was crying so hard that Mrs. Smith could not understand her. Mrs. Smith said, "Vicki, what's wrong?"

"I don't know, Mom, I just yelled at Antonio." Mrs. Smith said, "I'll be right over."

When Mrs. Smith arrived at the house, she could hear Vicki crying. She opened the door, walked in, wiped Vicki's eyes, and started hugging her.

"What's wrong, baby?"

"Mom, Antonio doesn't want me to go to California." "Baby, why are you going to California?"

"Oh, I haven't told you my good news. I have an agent that wants to meet with me at noon tomorrow."

"What?!! I'm so happy for you, this is the best news I have heard all day. Baby, you go right on up those stairs and finish packing your clothes. You let me deal with Antonio, I'm so proud of you. Don't you worry about a thing."

As Mrs. Smith was walking outside, she could see Antonio from far off, sitting in the park. As she was walking towards him, she noticed that he was crying. She sat down right beside him. Antonio looked at her so pitifully. "Hi, Mom, I guess your daughter called you."

"Yes, she did. Antonio, let me say something to you, and I want you to listen to me very carefully. Before I had Vicki, the doctor said that I would never have any children. So, I helped my two older sisters out with their children. I was the baby of the family. Everyone spent a lot of time with me. They gave me everything that I ever wanted, I was happy.

But I was also missing something: my very own child. Soon after I turned 24 years old, I met Vicki's father, he was fresh out of college, and we started dating. He wanted a child right away. And the hardest thing that I could have told that man was that I couldn't have a child. But one day I had to tell him. He was so understanding and he still wanted to marry me. After we got married, something that I never expected happened. I was pregnant with my only daughter. I had to stay in bed the whole nine months. I had a hard time. And ever since then, I never got pregnant again. That's why I gave her everything she wanted. She is the apple of her father's eyes. And now you both have given us grandbabies. This is my special blessing. So please, Antonio, don't blame Vicki for the way that she is acting right now. Blame me and her father."

Antonio replied, "I don't blame anyone, because I was giving her everything too. Well, Mrs. Smith, you have opened my eyes, so let me go back to my wife." As Antonio was walking away, he turned to Mrs. Smith and said, "Do you want to keep the boys tonight?"

Mrs. Smith jumped up and said, "Sure I do!!"

Antonio ran back into the house and picked Vicki up and said,

"I'm so sorry, baby, that I yelled at you and walked away." Antonio kissed her and helped her to finish packing. Vicki was so happy. When they were finishing up, the agent faxed Vicki her new contract and they made arrangements for her to stay in a hotel when she arrived in California. The agency also e- mailed her some information about her plane tickets, and who would be at the airport to meet her when she arrived the next day.

Antonio said, "Well, Vicki, this is finally it, you will be leaving without me in the morning. You'll be gone for three days, so I better spend all the time with you that I can."

Vicki was looking over her papers. Antonio took the contract out of Vicki's hands and said, "This is my time, just read it on the plane tomorrow."

Vicki began to laugh. Antonio took Vicki out to dinner. He wouldn't even talk about her trip. After they finished eating, Antonio wanted to go to the movies, but Vicki said, "Baby, that sounds good, but I have an early flight tomorrow," so they went back home. Antonio put on some soft music while he was changing out of his clothes. Vicki fell asleep. When he came back into the room, he just lay there and held his wife.

The next morning, when Vicki was getting ready, she asked Antonio to call her mother because she wanted to see her boys before she left. Antonio was putting her suitcases in the car. Vicki was rushing around trying to think of everything she would need. She didn't want to forget anything. Before they left, Vicki and Antonio picked up their boys to let them ride with her to the airport. The boys were so excited for their mom. All they could say was, "Mom you're going to ride the big plane." They did not understand the meaning of the trip. After they got to the airport, Vicki began to cry and said, "Antonio, I have never been without you since we've been married."

Antonio said, "I know, but it's just for three days and you will be running back into my arms."

Vicki went up to the front desk to get her tickets. Antonio said, "It's not too late to beg you to stay, is it?"

Vicki smiled and said, "I love you, Mr. Jackson."

Soon they were calling all the passengers to board flight 417. Vicki looked at her ticket and saw that it was her flight.

The boys were so excited to see the big planes. Vicki began to kiss Antonio. Then they called for everyone to board flight 417 for the last time. Vicki began to walk away from Antonio while blowing kisses to him and her boys. Antonio yelled out, "Wait, I have something for you!"

Vicki stopped in her very steps. Antonio ran over to her and put a necklace around her neck that had a locket, with a picture of the two boys together on one side and a picture of the two of them on the other. She really liked that. Then Vicki ran to board the plane. A stewardess was taking all of the tickets at the door of the plane and another was showing everyone their seats. Vicki had a first-class seat. She was so nervous and so excited that she didn't know what to do. While she was sitting in her seat, Vicki took out her contract and began to read it. She liked the offer that the agent offered her.

After reading the contract, she began to look through her handbag for a pen to sign it. She found a picture that her boys had drawn for her and it made her feel so special. She just smiled and thought about how blessed she was. She began to sign the papers.

After signing them, Vicki took the locket that Antonio gave her and just looked at it. By now she had been in the air for three hours, so Vicki relaxed and fell off to sleep. While she was resting, she was awakened by a loud thunderclap and flashes of lightning. Vicki and everyone else on the plane were scared. The pilot came on the intercom and told everyone to stay in their seats and make sure that their seatbelts were locked. The weather was just so bad. The pilot was trying to make an emergency landing. By the time the wind blew the plane right into a hurricane, everyone had begun to cry out for help. Vicki was so scared that she began to hold onto the necklace that Antonio had given her.

Something hit the door of the plane near Vicki's seat and the door came open. Vicki's seat was ejected from the plane. Nearly every bone in Vicki's body was broken from the pressure of being sucked out of the plane. Vicki's seat finally sailed across the top of some wooded area. She was barely alive as her seat sat at the top of a big tree. The limbs of the tree held her but also hid her from everyone. Vicki didn't even know that she was in this world.

By now, the air traffic control board at a nearby airport was trying to make contact but no avail. After the storm stopped, the UFC's were sent out to search for flight 417. As they discovered the crash, they found everyone was dead. The UFC's radioed back to the airport for them to get in touch with the families of everyone who was on flight 417, because there were no survivors. When it came on the news that flight 417 went down, and the newsperson was asking for family members to get to the airport as soon as possible, Antonio was at home with his sons but he was not watching the news. However, Mrs. Smith heard it and yelled out to Mr. Smith. "Honey, what flight did Vicki take?"

"I don't know, why don't you call Antonio and ask him? He will know." When Mrs. Smith called Antonio, there was no answer. Mr. Smith said, "Baby, let's go over to Antonio's house and when we get over there, I need you to keep it together. We don't want to scare the boys."

Mr. Smith didn't say a word when they arrived at Antonio's home. They saw Antonio outside playing with the boys. As they were getting out of their car, Antonio noticed the worried look on their faces.

As the Smiths walked over to Antonio, they asked him, "Could we speak to you alone?"

Antonio said, "Yes." Antonio told Antonio Jr. to take Ja'cob in the house and get ready for their bath. The boys kissed their grandma and grandpa and went into the house. Antonio checked to make sure that the boys could not hear them talk, then he turned to the Smiths and asked them,

"What's wrong?"

Mrs. Smith said, "Have you seen the news?" He answered, "No."

Then she said, "What flight did my daughter take this morning?"

"Flight 417."

Mrs. Smith fell to her knees and began to cry out, "Oh my God, my baby!"

Antonio heard the phone ringing; it was the people at the airport calling for a meeting.

Mr. Smith screamed, "Please don't tell me my baby's gone!" Antonio called his mother and father to tell them that he needed them to come over and watch the boys while he and the Smiths went to the airport. Once the Jacksons arrived, Antonio drove the Smiths to the airport with him. He was so nervous. Once at the airport, Antonio took off running for the doors. He couldn't even get close because there were already over three hundred people there trying to hear about their loved ones. The UFC's came into the room and began to call out everyone's name that was on flight 417. When they called out "Mrs. Vicki Jackson," Mrs. Smith held onto her husband and then they embraced Antonio. They all cried out for Vicki. Mrs.

Smith went into shock, and they had to call an ambulance to take her to the hospital because she couldn't speak and she wasn't responding to anyone's voice.

Antonio called his mom and dad and told them about Vicki, and he also told them not to tell the boys what had happened to their mother. Mr. Smith rode in the ambulance with his wife. As Antonio was arriving home, he could see cars lined up around the block.

So many people that knew him and Vicki were at his house. But his boys were upstairs and they didn't know what was going on. When Antonio walked into his home, he said to everyone, "Thank you so much for being here, but I'm so sorry I'm going to have to ask everyone to leave at this time. I have just learned about the news myself and I haven't yet sat down with my sons. So, I'm just asking everyone to give me some time."

The people understood. After everyone left, Mr. and Mrs. Jackson just held their son. When the boys heard them crying, they came running downstairs and saw their father on his knees crying. They ran over to him and said, "Dad, what's wrong?"

He turned to both of his sons and he said, "Boys, I have something to tell you. Tonight, your mother went home to heaven with the angels."

The boys didn't understand; They wanted their mother home with them. This was hard for the whole family and it was too much for Antonio to talk about. Antonio needed his mother and father to help him explain. Antonio was hurting so bad that he didn't know what to say. The family was so emotionally broken down. For days, Antonio could not sleep or eat anything. All he could do was cry out for Vicki. Antonio had this empty feeling from longing for his wife. At one point, Antonio would lay down at night and he would think that Vicki was coming through the door. The boys wouldn't sleep in their bed and would get in the bed with their father.

Antonio would just watch them sleep.

Three days had passed and Antonio went to his pastor. He wanted to have a funeral for Vicki. Pastor Tucker said, "Son, I think that would be a good idea." Pastor Tucker told him that he would set everything up. Antonio called their senior class to take part in the funeral. Pastor Tucker got with the family and that Sunday, after service was over, they went right into the funeral for Vicki. Mr. Smith came, but his wife was still in the hospital.

Antonio was talking to the congregation about how Vicki had empowered him to become the man that he was. Antonio was crying when the door opened. It was his older brother Ja'cob. Ja'cob walked over to Antonio and put his arms around him. They both began to cry as they were walking to their seats. Antonio's little boys were sitting like brave little boys. They didn't cry out loud, but tears were falling down their faces. They missed their mother.

After the funeral was over, the boys went home with Mr. and Mrs. Jackson. Mr. Smith went back to the hospital to be with his wife. She was still not talking. Antonio and Ja'cob just walked in the park where he and Vicki had spent a lot of time together. Antonio told Ja'cob that he was going to devote his time to raising his boys. Ja'cob asked him, "What about your business?"

Antonio said, "I really don't know, I haven't thought about that much."

Ja'cob gave Antonio a motivational talk. But Antonio looked back at Ja'cob as if he didn't have any life left in him. Antonio said he wanted Ja'cob to go with him to the crash site.

As Antonio and Ja'cob were walking through the park, Antonio noticed that two men were in his yard. They began to walk towards the men. The men were from the airport and they had come to give Antonio a check and Vicki's locket. The men told him how sorry they were for his loss. When Antonio saw the locket he cried out, "I guess this fixes everything!" Antonio was yelling at the two men. He kept saying, "My wife is gone!" Antonio fell to the ground holding Vicki's locket to his heart. The men repeated that they were so sorry for his loss. Ja'cob asked the men to leave as he was lifting his brother up from off the ground.

For four days, the news reported that flight 417 went down in a bad storm and there were no survivors. Antonio couldn't take anymore. He cut off the television. He had taken off from work to spend time with his sons. He had other people running the business. Antonio was also making preparations to go out to California to see the crash site. But the UFC's didn't clear him to go anywhere near the wreck. After the UFC's finished cleaning everything up, they left the area.

Vicki was still unconscious and her body was so broken, lying up on a tree. As she began to come to, she whispered so low, "Antonio, help me."

Antonio was asleep in his chair, and inside of himself, he heard her cry for him. He woke up thinking that it was a bad dream.

Meanwhile, out in California, it began to rain, and the more it rained, the more the branches released her body to the ground. Vicki knew that every breath that she took could be her last one. She was so wet and cold, out there all alone. But close by, there lived the most handsome Italian doctor, a man by the name of Matthew Collins. Dr. Collins was a young billionaire.

He was born and raised in Italy. He had inherited his father's empire. Dr. Collins moved from Italy to his father's twenty-five-thousand-acre estate. He finished college in Rome at no more than 28 years old, having majored in repairing the brain and plastic surgery. Dr. Collins also majored in repairing all parts of the body.

Dr. Collins' family was royalty. and he also had a mansion in Rome. He went all over the world teaching doctors his surgical system. He had inherited three hospitals in his father's name.

Every woman dreams of a man like this. People at the three hospitals glorified him because he was so nice to everyone. Dr. Collins was coming back to his estate from a two-week business meeting when he noticed that someone was lying on the ground next to one of his trees. When he approached the broken body, he saw that this lady was at the edge of dying. Dr. Collins was trying to figure out how this young lady got on his land. Vicki was still locked into her seat. Dr. Collins unloosened the seat belt and began to work on her. He checked Vicki's pulse and found that she was barely breathing.

She was bleeding from the back of her head, and many of her bones were broken. He called the hospital to report that he had found a woman on his land and she was hurt very badly. Not knowing that there had been a plane accident days before, Dr. Collins called for an ambulance to come out to his estate and then called the mansion and told his butler to open the gate for the rescue squad.

When the ambulance arrived at Collins Hospital, they rushed Vicki into surgery. Dr. Collins started washing up, and then he did everything that he could to save her. Dr. Collins stopped the bleeding from Vicki's brain, but she remained in a coma. Vicki lay in the hospital for nearly a year. Dr. Collins checked on her every day. She became his study. The nurses moved her around every day, but she was still unconscious.

Meanwhile, Antonio still found it hard to go on with his life. He was taking good care of his sons. Antonio Jr. had started school now and little Ja'cob was staying with Antonio's mother in the daytime. It had been a year since Vicki was gone. Antonio was back at work. Antonio's pastor came to him and asked him to help give the youth cookout that weekend. Antonio agreed. But Pastor Tucker never told

Antonio that he had a beautiful daughter that was going to be there. When Saturday came, Antonio volunteered to cook. While Antonio and the other men were cooking, the pastor walked over to everyone to introduce his daughter. Then Pastor Tucker and his wife sat down at the table with Mr. and Mrs. Jackson. He said, "It's a nice day, isn't it? Brother and Sister Jackson, let me ask you something."

"Okay, Pastor," Mr. Jackson replied cordially.

"You know that I love Antonio like a son, and now that Sister Vicki has been gone for a year, I really think that it's time for Antonio to move on with his life. Now, my Mary is fresh out of college and she could be a great wife to Antonio and a wonderful mother to his two sons. She won't try to take Vicki's place, but he needs someone. What do you both say?" The Jacksons agreed with their pastor. The Pastor concluded, "Well, let's do everything in our power to make that happen. I have already talked to my Mary."

Mary was walking around, meeting the other people. Mrs. Jackson jumped up and went to where Antonio was cooking. Mrs. Jackson said, "Antonio, let me introduce you to Mary, the pastor's daughter."

Antonio said, "No Mother, I'm not ready for this."

Mrs. Jackson said, "Son, it would make me very happy if you got to know Mary. Vicki is gone, plus she would want you to move on with your life." Mrs. Jackson finally convinced him to meet her. Antonio introduced himself to her, and they sat down at a table together and began to talk.

Antonio just wanted to be friends with her. They exchanged phone numbers, but he was in no way ready to date. After the cookout was over,

Antonio took his sons home. He put Mary's phone number in his address book, but he didn't call her. Soon his mother found out that

Antonio never called Mary. So, she gave a dinner at her house and had invited Mary as well as Antonio and his boys. Antonio went to his mother's dinner and saw Mary there. After dinner, Mrs. Jackson suggested that Antonio take Mary for a walk.

As they were walking, Mary was talking about her life. However, all Antonio could speak about was Vicki. But Mary listened to him and understood him. Mary was so amazed at how beautiful their neighborhood was. As a matter of fact, Mary's description of the neighborhood was the same as Vicki's. Antonio began to like her right away. He asked her out for the following weekend. The whole next week, Antonio and Mary called each other twice a day.

Other women wanted to go out with Antonio, but he had begun to like Mary more and more. Antonio and Mary got closer during the months to come. By now, Antonio felt safe enough to bring Mary around his sons. The boys were growing up and they wanted their father to be happy. Mary began to spend a lot of time with Antonio Jr. and little Ja'cob. After dating Mary for six months, Antonio surprised Mary at dinner one night when he asked her to marry him. Mary accepted his ring and said yes! Antonio was so happy that he didn't know what to do.

In that moment, Vicki woke up from her deep sleep. But she didn't know who she was, where she was, or where she came from. Then a nurse walked into her room and noticed that Vicki was awake. She ran down the hall to call Dr. Collins. Vicki was in so much pain. When Dr. Collins ran into the room, he began to ask her what her name was. Vicki didn't even know. Dr. Collins asked, "Do you remember anything?" Vicki said, "No."

Many days turned into weeks for Vicki in that hospital bed. She couldn't walk, and she couldn't even lift herself up. Dr. Collins wouldn't go home, he just stayed right there beside Vicki. Many of the administrators became concerned about Dr. Collins. But they would not say anything because he owned the hospital.

Many weeks came and went, and Vicki had such a hard time. One day, when Dr. Collins was not there a lady came into Vicki's room from the administrator's office to talk to her about her bill. As Dr. Collins was walking through the door, he yelled at the lady and told her to leave the room. He also told the woman to send the bill to him. She just said, "Yes,

Sir." Dr. Collins looked at Vicki and said, "I'm so sorry about that." Then he asked, "Have any of your memories come back?" Vicki said, "No."

Dr. Collins wanted to take Vicki back into surgery because she still had deep cuts on one side of her face. The next morning, he did major plastic surgery on the left side of her face. Every day, Dr. Collins and a physical therapist worked with Vicki to help her walk. She began to get stronger and stronger. After Vicki improved, Dr. Collins discharged her from the main hospital and sent her to a rehabilitation facility where she stayed for three months. When Vicki was nearing the end of her rehabilitation, Dr. Collins came in to watch her work out. Vicki was so happy to show him that she could walk by herself.

As she was showing off, she just about fell to the floor, but he caught her and they both started laughing. That's when he kissed her and she kissed him back. The head nurse saw them kissing, so she went to Dr. Collins and suggested that he discharge Vicki from rehab.

Dr. Collins said, "I'm going to give her one more week here."

The nurse sat down and talked to Vicki about what was getting ready to take place. On her last day at rehab, Vicki went to the head nurse and told her, "I don't know who I am or where I came from."

The nurse was preparing Vicki's discharge papers. She said, "Please wait before you leave because Dr. Collins needs to see you."

Dr. Collins was in a meeting with his administrators. Dr. Collins had a very good friend that worked with the United States Superior Court of California. His name was Jeff, and he was the best criminal lawyer in California. Dr. Collins called Jeff and explained to him what was going on. Jeff told Dr. Collins that he would take it before a judge to see what he would say, and that he would get back to him.

Jeff went to the head judge and told him what Dr. Collins had said. The judge requested that they take a picture of the young lady, and then put it on the news to see if anyone recognized her. He also requested that they give the young lady a name book and let her pick out a new name. The judge advised, "When she picks out her new name, just bring it back to my office and I will enter it in the court record, because she can't just walk out of here with no name."

The only one that Vicki trusted was Dr. Collins. When he took the name book to Vicki, they both began to pick out some names. Dr. Collins could see that Vicki was scared to leave the hospital. Her hands began to shake, so he took her hands in his and just held her. Then he began to joke around with her, and she began to laugh. As she was laughing, he just looked at her and smiled. They were both attracted to each other. He saw a name that he really liked. Amanda New was the name. She responded, "I like that name too."

Dr. Collins said, "Hello, Miss Amanda New." As Dr. Collins was watching Amanda, he took out his checkbook and said, "You are going to need some money." He wrote her a $5,000.00 check in the name of Amanda New.

She looked at him and said, "When I get my first job, I'm going to pay you back."

Dr. Collins said, "Amanda, don't leave yet. I need to call my friend Jeff, to give him your new name."

As she was sitting there, the nurse walked over to her and handed her some papers to get on the bus while saying, "Your bus number is

57 and it will take you to the Salvation Army where they are waiting for you. We will see you back here at the hospital in two weeks, but if you have any problems before then, you just come on back." After waiting awhile for Dr. Collins, she finally saw him come running back into the room with her new identity. After he gave her all of her paperwork, he just watched her walk away.

Amanda was waiting on her bus in front of the hospital, but the bus was so late that she drifted off to sleep on the bench. The bus came and then left her.

As Dr. Collins was leaving the hospital, he noticed that Amanda had fallen to sleep on the bench. He drove towards her and called her name three times. When she didn't wake up, he got out of his car and shook her until she woke up. He said, "Amanda, I believe that you have missed your bus." Amanda sat up and rubbed her eyes. As she looked up at Dr. Collins so sadly, he smiled at her and said, "You are so beautiful." She just smiled back at him. Dr. Collins said, "Come on, Amanda, I have a two-bedroom house on my estate. It's brand new; my father built it for me when I was a teenager, the time that I got out of hand. No one is using it, so you can have it as long as you like."

Amanda said softly, "Thank you so much."

Dr. Collins helped Amanda into his car. As they were leaving the hospital, that nurse that saw Dr. Collins kiss Amanda was standing at the hospital door and saw them pull off. She liked Dr. Collins herself.

But he didn't like her. As the good doctor was driving down the road, Amanda looked at him and asked him, "How long do you think it will be before I get my memory back?"

Dr. Collins said, "It may never return because of the trauma to your brain." Amanda didn't say anything else. She fell off to sleep. It took Dr. Collins an hour to get from the hospital to his estate. When

Amanda woke up, all she could see was these tall gates opening up. As Dr. Collins was driving through the gates, Amanda was in disbelief as she saw his big mansion. Dr. Collins said to Amanda, "Whatever you need, you just let me know."

She said, "Okay."

As Amanda was walking into her new home, Dr. Collins was showing her around. Then he said, "I will send one of my servants to help you out in the morning." As Dr. Collins was walking out the door, he turned and looked at her and said,

"Is everything okay?" "Yes, I'm just so tired." "Goodnight Amanda."

Amanda said, "Goodnight Dr. Collins."

He looked at her and he said, "I would love it if you called me Matthew." She smiled and said, "Okay."

Amanda was going from room to room. Finally, she took her bath and went to bed. As she was sleeping, she dreamt about two little boys calling for her, but she couldn't understand the dream. The dream woke her up and she couldn't get back to sleep, so she just lay in that bed crying because she felt like someone needed her.

The next morning, at daybreak, Amanda was sitting beside the window, feeling empty, listening to the birds singing.

Then a knock came at the door. When she opened it, it was the butler from the mansion saying that Dr. Collins requested her presence at the main house for breakfast.

As she was walking toward the mansion, she saw Dr. Collins standing in the doorway, waiting for her. As she stepped into the mansion, Dr. Collins took her by the hand and led her into the sunroom to eat. As she entered the room, she turned to Dr. Collins and said, "Dr. Collins, you don't have to do this."

"Please, Amanda, call me Matthew, and I know that I don't have to do this, but I want to. You mean a great deal to me." "But this is too much."

"Please sit down," he said and pulled her chair out for her. As they began to eat, she noticed that he was looking at her with this big smile. After they finished eating, Dr. Collins offered Amanda a walk on his estate. She accepted the walk with him. As she was going through his living room, this big picture on his wall caught her full attention. She turned to him and she asked him, "Who is she? She is very beautiful."

"That's my mother, she and my stepdad live in Pakistan." "What happened to your real father?"

"My mother left him for her new husband and he killed himself." "Oh, I should not have asked you that. I'm so sorry."

"That's okay, I'm glad that I have someone to talk to." As he was walking over to her, he took his hand and put it around her shoulder and then he kissed her. Dr. Collins looked into Amanda's eyes and said, "You have the most beautiful eyes, you have the eyes of a dove."

Amanda took him in her arms and held him. As they were standing and looking at each other's eyes, he took her by the hands and led her into his bedroom. When they entered the room, Dr. Collins kissed Amanda very passionately. He picked her up and laid her down on his bed. As they undressed each other, Dr. Collins reached over and got his bottle of Love Savoir Ointment. He applied it all over her body. As he kissed and rubbed her body all over, he whispered in her ears, "You are mine." Then he laid his body on top of her and made love to her. She felt as if she was in Paradise, coming out of the bed of Pleasure. After making love, they both curled up into each other and then went to sleep in each other's arms. About two hours later, they both got up and dressed. Dr. Collins asked Amanda to move in with him and she said yes. Amanda moved in with him that very day.

They had lived together for no more than two months when Dr. Collins went to Amanda and asked her to marry him. As she was looking at him she said, "You are the most handsome bachelor that I have ever met. Yes, I will marry you."

In that very hour, he took her back into Paradise as he made love to her. In that very moment of pleasure, Amanda conceived, but she didn't know it. Amanda went to sleep, but Dr. Collins got up, dressed, and went to the butler and all of his servants and told them that Amanda should not be awakened by anyone. Dr. Collins told the butler that he was going into town. As he was leaving, Amanda woke up and saw him going out of the gate. So she put on her clothes and walked through the garden. The butler called Dr. Collins on his cell phone and told him that Amanda woke up and was walking in the garden. Dr. Collins responded, "Okay. I'll be back very soon."

Dr. Collins went to town to buy Amanda an engagement ring. After Dr. Collins picked out the most beautiful ring he saw for her, he went back to his estate. As he was walking towards her, he saw her sitting in the garden. He got down on one knee and said, "Will you marry me?" Then he put the ring on her finger. Amanda looked at the ring and she began to cry. As she was kissing him, she said yes, again. As they were sitting in the garden of flowers, they began to set the date. Dr. Collins wanted to get married right away.

Amanda said, "We haven't picked you out a suit, nor have I picked out my wedding dress."

Dr. Collins said, "Don't you worry about anything. I'm having people out here this afternoon to fit you for your dress, and I bought my suit when I went to town."

Amanda said, "Matthew, this is the happiest day of my life! But I don't have anyone to invite to my own wedding."

"Don't worry about that either because I'm not that close to anyone myself. I just have a few faithful friends."

As the weeks went by, Dr. Collins began to spend all of his time with Amanda. He also grew extremely jealous over her. He wouldn't let her talk to any of the male servants. He watched over her as if someone was going to take her away from him. They were spending so much time together that Dr. Collins began to teach Amanda how to speak Spanish and French. Her loyalty was to him and him alone.

One day he wanted to walk on his estate with Amanda, but as she was getting ready to walk with him, she began to feel very sick. He went into the room where Amanda was and checked her.

He discovered that they were going to have a baby. They both were so happy. That's when they both agreed to move up the wedding date. Dr. Collins brought in top-notch wedding planners, and he called his friends and family. His friends and family couldn't understand why he was in such a rush to marry a black woman. They knew that he was extremely powerful and a very popular doctor, so they didn't say anything to him.

On the day of their wedding, the news media and many celebrities were there. They had a Cinderella-type wedding, and people came from all over the world to see it. Amanda looked like a princess. Dr. Collins stood like a soldier, feeling very secure, and he never took his eyes off of her as she walked toward him.

Months later, after Amanda came to the end of her nine months, Dr. Collins delivered their baby girl. Dr. Collins named their daughter Beth Collins.

Beth weighed seven pounds. By now, Dr. Collins had become obsessed over Amanda. Anywhere Amanda walked, he was nearby, just like her shadow.

He wouldn't even let Amanda go to the bathroom by herself,

but she thought that was funny. As time was going by, little Beth was growing up. For her first birthday, Dr. Collins gave her the biggest birthday party that any little girl could ever dream of. Little Beth was a daddy's little girl. After Beth's big party, and everyone had gone home, Amanda and Dr. Collins were lying on the floor of their living room, playing with Beth. Matthew kept watching Amanda. It wasn't long before he moved over to where she was and began to kiss her. And then he sent for one of his handmaids to get Beth. As the handmaid was getting Beth, Dr. Collins took Amanda into the bedroom. He made love to her gently.

Dr. Collins never went back to the hospital. He just spent more and more time with Amanda and little Beth. It wasn't long before Amanda was pregnant again. Amanda got sick one morning and he took some blood work from her. He found that it was positive because he had his own lab in that big mansion. They both were so happy about the new baby that was coming because they felt little Beth needed someone to play with. Beth was so precious to both of them. Everything was going so well.

Late in Amanda's pregnancy, she had that dream again about two little boys who were crying for her. She woke up out of her sleep crying for them again. When she went to Dr. Collins about it, he looked at her and said, "You have only one child, that is our little Beth." And he didn't say anything else about it. Since she didn't want to upset him, she didn't bring it up again. Two weeks later, Amanda went into labor and she had another little girl. Dr. Collins named her Angel Collins Dr. Collins was so proud of his family. Angel weighted eight pounds. She was a big healthy baby.

Amanda went to her husband to talk to him about tying her tubes but he said, "No, I want to try to have a son later."

While they were talking, Dr. Collins' mother showed up. She had just walked into the mansion, and when he saw her, she was already standing in his living room, so he yelled out, "How did you get past those gates?"

"What happened, son? You must have forgotten that I used to live here with you and your father. Oh, I see that you haven't changed at all."

As his mother was walking and looking all around, Dr. Collins yelled at her, "Mother, what do you want?"

"Well, I see that my model, who called himself a doctor, has went to the lost and found to get himself a black woman. I find this to be a problem for me, because now you have made me a grandmother of two little girls that I have never seen."

Then she said, "Oh, did my special invitation get lost in the mail? Because I saw you two all over the news." Amanda didn't know what to say. Dr. Collins looked at Amanda and then looked back at his mother. He said, "Mother, get out." She said, "Not before I meet my grandchildren."

It was so hard for Amanda to watch them yell at each other. Dr. Collins' mother walked over to the wall and began to take the children's picture off of it. Dr. Collins called for the butler to put his mother out. As he was taking her to the door, she yelled back at Amanda and she said, "I feel so sorry for you, because you haven't seen the real Matthew. He is just like his father, a very deadly man, Amanda. You will never be able to leave this place. He doesn't want you to have a mind of your own."

Dr. Collins jumped up and pushed his mother out the door. Amanda ran over to her husband and held him as he fell into her arms. Dr. Collins' mother was going to her car with the children's picture in her hands.

She yelled at Amanda, "You just wait until he goes crazy and holds you in captivity and won't let you go." Amanda cried out, "Will you just leave? And please don't come back!"

Dr. Collins said to Amanda, "This lady has never loved my father, she just used him. The only reason that she married him and had me, is because my dad came from a very wealthy family in Italy. When I was 15 years old,

Mother left my dad for another man and my dad couldn't go on without her, so my dad took a gun and he shot himself in front of me." Amanda held her husband and comforted him until he stopped crying. That was the first time that she had ever seen him cry. She tried to calm him down. His heart was broken. Amanda suggested that they take the children and go away for a little while. Dr. Collins liked that. He said, "I have a surprise for you, I was going to wait, but this would be a good time for me to give you the gift that I have bought you. Get your things together, and I'll take you and the girls away from here for a while. But right now, I want you to open up your gift." It was a matching set of diamond and ruby earrings and a necklace.

Amanda loved it, and she asked him, "What is this for?"

"You have never had a birthday party or anything, so today is your birthday."

Amanda loved the jewelry but she wanted to know when was her real birthday. Dr. Collins said, "Well, the judge didn't give you one."

Amanda said, "Baby, where are we going?"

Dr. Collins said, "It's a big surprise." Then he called the handmaids in and told them to pack some clothes for Beth and baby Angel. And then he called the pilot and told him to fuel the jet. As Amanda was packing, Dr.

Collins walked over to her and said, "Amanda if you ever left me, I would be devastated, because you are my inspiration. I realized that I couldn't make it without you, you are so perfect in so many ways." Amanda looked at him and said, "I will never leave you," she said, then added, "You know what you need – a social life." He began to laugh at what she had said. As they were leaving the mansion, Dr. Collins handed Amanda some keys. "Honey, what do these keys fit?"

He started laughing and he said, "You will see."

Dr. Collins also took three of his servants with them. He was asleep, but little Beth was playing all over her dad. Dr. Collins took Amanda and his girls to London, where he had bought Amanda a ten-bedroom mansion. He gave Amanda the deed to the mansion. Their first night in London, the cook made gourmet meals. Little Beth just ran and played until she fell off to sleep in her father's arms. He just watched her sleep. They lived in London for eight months, and everything was wonderful until the administration contacted Dr. Collins to tell him that the ten doctors that he had hired were coming in three weeks and he needed to be back in California. He agreed to return. Then he went into the room where Amanda was reading a book to Beth and he said, "Baby, let the handmaid do that. I need to talk to you."

But Beth yelled out to him and she said, "No, Dad, I want my mom to read to me."

So, he laughed and said, "Okay, Beth."

After Amanda finished reading, Beth got her doll and she lay down with her. As they were going into the next room, Amanda said, "What's wrong, baby?"

He said, "We are going to have to fly out soon, go back to California, because I have an obligation to the hospital."

"I know, but I love it here."

"I know, we may be able to come back soon after I interview these ten doctors."

Amanda said, "Okay, when are we leaving?"

"Not tonight, you have me all to yourself." She took him by the hand and pulled him into the bedroom where they made love. They both went off to sleep and the handmaid rocked little Angel to sleep, but Beth was already asleep in her bed. A few days later, Dr. Collins and his family packed up and moved back to their mansion in California. After they got back home, Dr. Collins set up appointments to meet the new doctors. He called home to let Amanda know that he was going to be late and to hold dinner for him.

Dr. Collins also told Amanda that he was going to be heading a conference in New York in about a week and that he wanted her to go with him.

She said, "Let's talk about it when you come home."

"Okay, but I will be out of here soon, because I'm not going to do all ten interviews today."

"Well, I'll see you soon." As she was hanging up the phone, little Beth wanted to dance, so Amanda cut the radio on. Beth began to jump and hop around. Amanda began to dance with her. Beth wanted her mother to turn the radio up. One of the handmaids walked up to Amanda and said, "Mrs. Collins, I don't mean any harm, but the music is waking up little Angel."

Amanda said, "Thank you very much, but it is time for Angel to get up anyway, plus these are my children and this is my home!" The handmaid walked out of the room. Amanda was still playing with Beth, and then she woke up Angel. Angel had just learned how to walk, and she began to play with her sister. A beautiful song came on and Amanda told Beth to hold her around her legs and dance with her.

Amanda picked Angel up and she was kissing her, and then she put her close to her heart and began to dance slowly with both of them.

Dr. Collins came up early, and when he heard the music playing as he was walking into the mansion, he just stood there smiling at them. Amanda didn't see him; she had her eyes closed. So, he walked in and quietly joined in the dance. As he was taking little Angel from out of Amanda's arms, he noticed that she had been crying. As he looked into her eyes, he called for one of the handmaids to come and get the children and take them to their room. As the handmaid took the girls to their playroom, the music was still playing and Dr. Collins turned to Amanda and asked her for a dance. As they were slow dancing, he kissed her and she put her head on his shoulder. Then he told her, "Amanda Collins, I love you with all my heart, mind, body, and soul." She just looked at him and smiled. Then he said, "That smile is what melted my heart when you woke up from that deep sleep." He just kept on kissing her. Finally, he took her into the bedroom and made love to her slowly.

After they finished making love, she asked Dr. Collins, "When are you going to tie my tubes?" "Let's wait until the girls get to be four years old and five years old, because I want to try for a boy. After I have my son, then I will tie your tubes." Amanda didn't say anything, she just lay there, but he went to sleep.

The next morning, Dr. Collins was still asleep, but Amanda had risen and got dressed, and she told her handmaid to get the girls ready. Amanda did something she had never done before: she called for a driver to come around the front of the mansion. When the car pulled around, Amanda told the driver to take her to town. The driver said, "Mrs. Collins, I need to clear this with Dr. Collins because I could lose my job." She said, "You will lose it if you don't take me."

He said, "You are the lady."

As they were leaving, Dr. Collins had rolled over to hug Amanda but found she was not there. When he put on his housecoat, he realized that neither Amanda nor his daughters were there. He rushed into his room to put on his clothes; so many things were going through his mind.

As Amanda's driver paused at a stop sign, Amanda heard this beautiful song that a choir was singing. She asked her driver to pull over to the church. Amanda got her girls and they went into the church. Meanwhile, her driver stood outside the car, but then he turned the radio off and went into the church too. Dr. Collins was trying to get the driver on his radio but got no answer. Now Dr. Collins was going out of his mind. Dr. Collins was ordering his staff to tell him where his family went, but all they could tell him was that Mrs. Collins said that she was going into town. Then he called his other driver to take him into town to find them. The driver was going so fast that he did not look over at the church when he passed it. He went into town, but he could not find them. By now Dr. Collins was so mad that he didn't know what to do. So he asked the driver to take him back home. When he got back to the mansion, neither Amanda nor his children were there. One hour after he got back home, Amanda and his daughters came pulling up. Dr. Collins was sitting outside waiting for them. As they were getting out of the car, Beth ran to her father and said, "Dada, we went to church and we had a good time."

Amanda was holding Angel. Dr. Collins called for one of his handmaids to get his daughters. The handmaid took Angel from out of Amanda's arms and took Beth from Dr. Collins. Dr. Collins was standing with his arms folded, just looking at Amanda. When Dr. Collins saw that the girls were in the mansion, he began to yell at Amanda and her driver. "Where did you two go with my babies?" He ran down the steps and hit Amanda in the face. He was yelling and cursing at Amanda and her driver. He accused them of sleeping together. Amanda was holding her face and she cried, "Matthew, what is wrong with you?" Dr. Collins fired the driver. Amanda said, "Please don't fire him, he only did what I asked him." As she was trying to explain herself, he ran into her and pushed her to the ground. Then he started dragging her into the mansion. Amanda was pleading and trying to get

away from him. He wouldn't listen to anything she was saying. He was hurting her real bad. All she could do was cry out for help. The driver began to yell at Dr. Collins, but he said to him, "You don't want to come up against me."

The head housekeeper walked outside and told him to leave, but everyone was so scared for her that they didn't say anything.

Dr. Collins yelled out, "Amanda, you slept with him, didn't you?" "No!"

"Tell me, Amanda, if you slept with him!"

"No! I didn't sleep with him."

Then he picked her up by the neck and took her into his mansion and threw her into a closet. Dr. Collins slammed the door and locked it from the outside. Then he fell down to the floor crying out Amanda's name. Amanda was in the closet calling out for someone to help her. Then Dr. Collins started saying, "Amanda if you leave me, I will kill you!"

Amanda was so scared, her face and throat hurt and her legs were bleeding. He left her locked in that closet for over three hours. Finally, she just lay down on the floor. The butler called Jeff, Dr. Collins' best friend, and he told him to come over because Dr. Collins needed him. When Jeff arrived, he ran into the mansion and picked Dr. Collins up from the floor. Jeff talked him into letting Amanda out of the closet.

When Dr. Collins opened the door. Amanda was down on her knees. She slowly looked up at him with tears running down her face. He tried to help her up, but she pushed him away. As she was walking away from him, she collapsed onto the floor. He ran over to her to check her pulse. He then examined her and found out that her blood pressure was up and that she was pregnant again. When Amanda came to, Dr. Collins was sitting beside the bed and Jeff was sitting in a chair close by. Amanda was so upset with her husband, and she said, "Matthew, you told me you would never hit me, but you dragged me down like a dog in front of my babies and the whole staff. Matthew, you broke my heart, and you scared me."

All Dr. Collins could do was just cry. He said, "Please don't ever, ever leave me."

"I would have never dreamed of this, Matthew. I stood right beside you when your mother said all of those bad things about you. I have honored you, but you have dishonored me." Matthew, I didn't see that I was in bondage because you made it look too good. But I'm no more than one of your servants, the only thing is that I share your bed and have your children.

How could you accuse me of having sex with one of your drivers? And let me ask you something else, while I'm on this thing, are our daughters in bondage too?"

Dr. Collins said, "No! Those are my children. I love you with my whole heart Amanda."

Amanda was trying to get up, but she didn't have the strength or the courage to do it. She just lay there looking at her husband. Dr. Collins got onto the bed and lay there beside her. He said to her, "My obligation is to you and my children and these hospitals, and I just can't let anything come between us."

Amanda took Dr. Collins by his hand and she said, "Baby, don't you know that I love you? I'm so sorry that I hurt you and made you feel like you couldn't trust me. I will never leave this place again, without you knowing it."

Dr. Collins said, "I do trust you. I just can't stand to think that you will leave me."

Jeff stood up and said, "I'm getting ready to go, because you don't need me right now. I'm glad you both are talking, and congratulations on your new baby that is on the way."

Amanda said, "Jeff, what do you mean?"

Dr. Collins began to laugh and he said, "Oh, I didn't tell you. When you fainted, I examined you and you are two months pregnant."

Amanda said, "Oh no, this is your doing, Matthew." and they both began to laugh.

Jeff said, "I will show myself out." As Jeff was leaving, the butler walked outside to thank him. Meanwhile, Dr. Collins picked Amanda up and put her on top of him. They laid there like that until both of them fell asleep. Two hours later, Dr. Collins woke up then watched Amanda sleep for a few minutes. Then he got up and went into the next room to prepare his speech for the next day in New York City. Amanda was still sleeping and she has the dream of two boys calling her for the third time. But this time Amanda could see their little faces as they were crying for her. She began to scream out to them, then she began to cry for them.

In the next room, Dr. Collins heard her cry and he jumped up and ran into the next room to help his wife, just to find her still asleep. When he reached out to wake her up, he listened to her as she talked in her sleep. He heard her call out the names Ja'cob and Antonio Jr. That worried him, because he didn't know anyone by those names. So, he sat down on the bed beside her and thought out loud, "Could these be her boys that she's dreaming about?" Then he shook her to wake her up.

Amanda was crying when she woke up and she said, "Honey, I had that dream again about those two little boys. Baby, what do you think that this dream is trying to tell me?"

Dr. Collins said, "I don't know." Then he changed the subject.

"It will make me so happy if you go with me to New York tomorrow."

Amanda said, "No baby, this is a business trip that you are making tomorrow and I don't want to get in your way. I'll just stay here with the girls." But soon he convinced her to go. As she was lying in the bed, the girls were playing in the next room and then they ran into the room to see their mother sitting up and Dr. Collins laughing and talking with her.

One of the handmaids ran in after them, but by now Beth and Angel were on top of the bed with Amanda. Dr. Collins turned to the handmaid and said, "Let them spend some time with their mother."

The handmaid responded, "Yes, sir" and she went away.

Amanda and Dr. Collins were playing on the bed with the girls, and little Beth said, "Dad, we don't want to sleep in our beds tonight, we want to sleep with you and Mom in this big bed?"

Dr. Collins said, "Ask your mom, Beth." Amanda said, "Yes, Why not?"

Dr. Collins went into the other room to finish up his speech. He could hear Beth and Angel laughing as Amanda told them a story she had made up.

Beth said, "Mom, you tell good stories." Amanda said, "Oh yeah?"

Dr. Collins sent one of his handmaids to go out to the store to pick out some clothes for Amanda for her two-day trip in New York. The next day, Amanda and Dr. Collins were going on as if nothing was wrong.

They were laughing and talking, getting ready to leave for New York. Dr. Collins was making sure that everything was all right with the jet. While he was doing that, Amanda was talking to the keeper of the mansion and the babysitters. Dr. Collins walked back into the room and he kissed the girls then Amanda kissed them. As they were leaving, Amanda began to cry for the girls. After they boarded the jet to New York, Dr. Collins was reading over his notes.

Amanda began to read a book. The book was one of the best-selling children's books by Mrs. Vicki Jackson. As she was reading it, she couldn't help but feel that she knew her. At the end of the book, there was a passage about how Mrs. Vicki Jackson's life had ended, and about her husband, Antonio Jackson, and the two little boys that she had left behind. When Amanda read that, she remembered that she had a dream about two boys with the same names Mrs. Jackson's sons had. Amanda said, "Matthew, look at this book. This may be why I keep dreaming about those boys."

Dr. Collins said, "What do you mean?"

"Lately, I've been ordering a lot of books and I've ordered all four of Mrs. Jackson's books. I have been reading them to the girls."

He stopped doing what he was doing and looked at the book. Dr. Collins said, "It would have been nice if they had put the pictures of the family in the book, so the world could see them."

Then he gave the book back to Amanda, and she said, "All four of her books hit the best-seller list. This has got to be hard on her children."

Dr. Collins looked at Amanda when she said that, then commented, "One thing I know is, you could write children's books yourself, because I love the children's stories that you make up for the girls." That made Amanda feels good when he said that. She reached over and kissed him. Then she went back to reading.

It wasn't long before the pilot said, "Dr. Collins, we are arriving in New York. Please make sure you and your wife are locked in your seats." Amanda looked at Dr. Collins with this wary look, and he said to her, "Baby, everything is fine. I'm here with you and I'm not going to let anything happen to you." Amanda just sat there silently until they landed.

Dr. Collins had a car waiting for them at the airport and the driver took them to the hotel. After they arrived at the hotel, Dr. Collins had no more than two hours to get ready for the conference, and as they were changing their clothes, Dr. Collins walked over to Amanda and got on one knee. He began to kiss her stomach, and he looked up at Amanda and said with a smooth tone, in a voice so low, "You are my dove, and tonight I'm going to take you to a five-star restaurant and we are going to have a special dinner." And then he said, "We have never taken a cruise together, so when I get everything in order, let's take one." Amanda agreed. When they arrived at Sun Prairie Inn for the conference, doctors from all over the world and many medical students were there to hear about Dr. Collins' research on repairing the brain. As Dr. Collins and Amanda were walking into the conference room, the response was overwhelming: everyone stood up and applauded for him. The place was packed. There were news reporters all over the place. Amanda had a reserved seat in the front row. As he walked his wife to her seat, Dr. Collins kissed her in front of everyone. When he walked to the front of the dais, Dr. Collins had this assurance about himself as he looked around at the people.

Amanda was so happy for him. As Dr. Collins was doing his presentation, he began to talk about his experience with repairing the brain. He said, "First of all, I am a professor of the whole body." Then he explained how his practice had taken him into the unexplored regions of the brain. As he was talking, he just kept on watching Amanda. He talked for over one hour, and as he was coming to a close, he said, "To the great people of this conference, I submit to you one of my greatest accomplishments, my wife Amanda Collins." Then he began to project onto a screen picture of her broken body, and pictures of her brain. All the while, he explained in medical terminology how he made her whole again. Amanda didn't know what to say when he did that.

He walked over to her and he whispered in her ear, "Stand up and smile for the people." Amanda was trying to smile but that was the first time that she had ever seen those pictures. Amanda almost went into shock. Everyone was clapping and they began to talk loudly. Amanda just played it off and sat down again.

After he finished talking, he asked Amanda, "Where do you want to eat?" Amanda was speechless. Amanda began to wave goodbye to the people as they were leaving. As they were walking out the door, Dr. Collins said, "Let me call that five-star restaurant to reserve our seats."

"No, I'm going back to the hotel, you and I need to talk," Amanda said

He walked over to Amanda and said, "People are looking, you better not make a scene."

When they got back to their hotel. Dr. Collins kept on trying to kiss her, but she kept pushing him away. Amanda was so upset, she told him that she wanted to go home. Dr. Collins turned and looked at her and said, "This is just like you." He began to yell at her. "Run, Amanda, like you always do!" Then he walked out the door and slammed it behind him. Amanda ran into the bathroom and she threw up. After she came out of the bathroom, she kept crying.

Dr. Collins met some doctors that were in town for the conference. He went out with them and stayed out until the next morning. Amanda didn't sleep at all. She kept thinking about those pictures.

The next morning when Dr. Collins came back to the hotel, Amanda wasn't there. She got up very early, took some money from an ATM machine, got her belongings, and moved to another hotel.

Dr. Collins could not find her. He went running to the front desk and the clerk told him that she had checked out early that morning. Dr. Collins said, "Did she say where she was going?"

"No sir, she didn't."

Dr. Collins went running out of the building. He checked every store and every hotel, but he could not find her. Dr. Collins realized that New York was a big city and Amanda had never been there alone. As he was looking for her, he stopped to call back home to check on the girls. One of his new servants answered the phone and Dr. Collins said, "Listen, this is Matthew Collins, I'm calling to check on my babies." The servant said, "Just like I have told Mrs. Collins, the girls are doing fine."

"What, you talked to my wife?" "Yes, sir."

"Did she tell you what hotel she was staying in?"

The servant said, "No, sir, I thought that she was with you."

"Something happened and she left, but is there any way that you can check the caller ID to see where she was calling from?"

The servant said, "Yes." Then she checked for the number, and yelled out, "Oh, Dr. Collins, I have it!"

He took the number and said, "Thank you."

After the servant hung up the phone, she began to whisper to another servant that something had gone wrong with the Collinses in New York.

The news went all over the mansion. One of the servants said, "Mrs. Collins should be grateful to have him. He brought her from death's door and he gave her all of this. She lives like a princess. The things that I could get used to, yes, I could really enjoy this." Miss Rose, the head housekeeper opened up the door and all the servants got scared because Miss Rose had the power to fire every one of them. Miss Rose said, "You all get back to work." And then she yelled at the servant that had taken the phone calls from Dr. Collins and Mrs. Collins and then told everyone what was happening.

Miss Rose told her that if it ever happened again, she would lose her job. Meanwhile, Dr. Collins had found the hotel that Amanda was staying in. He had his driver take him to her hotel, but he didn't get out and had his driver park right in front of the hotel. He was sitting in the car waiting for her to come out. Amanda was in her room asleep. She had been up all night. Finally, she got up and looked out of her window to see that it was a day like no other. After she took her shower and got dressed, she was walking through the lobby when she noticed two little boys walking with their father. As she was getting ready to check out, she noticed that the father kept looking at her. She was standing right behind them, but the boys never looked her way, so she didn't see their faces. She just smiled at the man but didn't say anything to him. As she was walking out the door, she noticed that one of the boys dropped their toy. Amanda picked it up in front of the hotel and she yelled to the child, "Little boy, you dropped your toy…" As she was handing it to him, both boys turned to her and she cried out, "Antonio Jr. and little Ja'cob!"

Antonio turned around real fast and looked at her, and then he said, "It can't be true," and he rushed over to her and took her by her right hand.

He turned it over to see if she had the birthmark that Vicki had on the side of her hand, and she did. That was one thing that Dr. Collins could not change. By this time, Dr. Collins jumped out of the car, ran over to her, and forced her into his car. He demanded that the driver take them straight to the airport. He radioed the pilot to get the jet ready to leave. Amanda was fighting to get free from him. She hit him in the mouth and he began to bleed. He got so mad that he smashed her head up against the window, which knocked Amanda out. Blood had gotten onto his shirt, but he closed his jacket so no one could see it.

Meanwhile, Antonio had written down his tag number from the car and he called the police. When the police arrived, Antonio tried so hard to explain himself to the officer. The officer took the license number into the station and, when it came back, the officer got out of his car and said to Antonio, "You must be mistaken, that could not have been your wife, these are powerful people."

Antonio said, "Sir, that was my wife, Vicki Jackson. She may look a little different because she was in a plane accident."

The officer gave Antonio a disapproving look and said, "Sir, I don't have time for this," and the officer left. There was a doctor that was coming out of the hotel who overheard Antonio saying that Mrs. Collins was his wife. The doctor walked over to him and said, "Sir, I heard what you said to that officer. If you go into that hotel right there, you will find pictures still resting on the dais of Mrs. Collins before plastic surgery and after her surgery. I don't know why Dr. Collins didn't take them with him."

Antonio ran into the building with his two boys and, what he saw as he was looking at the pictures, he just could not believe. The before picture looked just like Vicki, but half of her face was crushed, and the after picture looked nothing like her. The doctor that told Antonio to go into the building finally walked in and said, "You know, I'm an expert in plastic surgery, but I can do nothing like this. Dr. Collins is the best of his time." Then the doctor left. Antonio took the pictures and left New York with them. He was very grievous in his spirit about these pictures and how the officer did not believe him and Dr. Collins carried Vicki away.

Antonio called Mr. Smith when he landed back in North Carolina, then went straight to his house with those pictures. Mr. Smith had retired after Vicki's accident and he stayed home to care for his wife. Mrs. Smith never said another word after she learned Vicki had died, she just lay there with a nurse helping her. As Antonio was walking up, he didn't knock on the door but just ran into the Smiths' home. Mr. Smith jumped up and said, "What's the matter, son?"

Antonio said, "Dad, you are not going to believe this, but your daughter is still alive!"

"What did you say, Antonio?" Antonio showed him the before and after pictures. Mr. Smith cried out, "Oh my God, my baby!"

Antonio said, "Dad, it's going to be hard trying to get her back, because she is married to one of the wealthiest men in the world."

Mr. Smith said, "This is my daughter and she is coming home." Then they went to the Internet to pull up Dr. Collins. They saw so much information on Dr. Collins: where he got his bachelor's degree, how he majored in repairing the brain, and even how much wealth he had.

Antonio found just a little on his, wife, Amanda, and their two daughters. Antonio looked at Mr. Smith and he said, "It looks like you have two more grandbabies." Mr. Smith was reading right along with Antonio, and then he looked back at Vicki's picture. As they were searching the Internet, information also came up on how Dr. Collins was looking for the family of a young lady that could not remember who she was, about a year and six months after Vicki's accident.

"How could we have missed all of this information, Dad?"

"For one thing, Vicki looks like a totally different woman. We could have looked at her all day and not known who she was, and UFC's said that no one survived that crash. Didn't they give you back that locket that you gave Vicki right before she boarded the plane?" Now, Antonio didn't know what to say. Then Mr. Smith said,

"Son, this is a miracle to me. My daughter is alive!" Then, he started whispering, "Oh, I don't want my wife to know anything about this until we bring Vicki home safely."

"I agree, because if we make one mistake, we could lose her for good." "Antonio, what do you mean?"

"Read this. Dr. Matthew Collins has two other hospitals in two other countries and he also inherited two other mansions in those countries from his father's estate. So, if he thinks that we are coming after him, he could leave California forever and take Vicki and their children with him."

Mr. Smith said, "Antonio, do you think that Vicki remembers anything about us?"

"I don't think so, but she does remember the boys. She looked at me as if I was a stranger right before Dr. Collins threw her into that car."

"Why did he throw her into a car?"

"It looked like they were having some problems. Mr. Smith, I'm going to put some information on the Internet and hopefully someone will see it and get it to her."

Mr. Smith said, "Aren't you scared that Dr. Collins may see it?"

"No, because he doesn't know that I got his tag number, and he doesn't know anything about us."

Mr. Smith said, "Antonio, I have always liked you, and I have always wanted your children to be happy, but I must say, I'm so glad that you didn't marry the pastor's daughter."

"I'm glad that I didn't marry her either, because that wouldn't be right. I didn't love her. She was nice and everything, but you just can't replace people with other people, because that wouldn't be right. Plus, I left everything the way that Vicki had left it, and I just couldn't have anyone touching her things." Then Antonio said, "I'm getting ready to call Ja'cob, my brother, because he is the best lawyer in New York City, and he will come through for me."

Dr. Collins had made it to his jet. He didn't have to check into the airport, so he had the driver drive right up to his jet. Amanda was still unconscious. The pilot helped Dr. Collins put Amanda on the jet and Dr. Collins told him to be careful because she was pregnant. Then he told the driver to go back to the hotel to get his clothes. After Dr. Collins landed on his estate, he took

Amanda in his arms and just held her. He then called his butler and told him to take his daughters for a thirty-minute ride away from his estate and clear everyone out of the mansion.

The butler said, "As you wish, I will do this right away."

Then Dr. Collins radioed the pilot and told him to just leave and not tell anyone what he saw. He gave the pilot a lot of money, and the pilot left. The butler radioed Dr. Collins back and told him, "Everything is cleared and I have your daughters on the road." Dr. Collins walked off the plane with Amanda in his arms, and as he was walking, he cried out, "Amanda, I will never let you leave me!" As Dr. Collins walked into the mansion, he took Amanda into a soundproof room that no one knew anything about. He laid Amanda down on this big bed, then began to take off all her clothes.

Amanda began to wake up, and he stood over her and said, "Amanda, we need to talk."

Amanda refused to listen to anything that he had to say. Amanda was in a daze. She was looking around as she said, "Matthew, where am I? And where are my daughters?"

Dr. Collins was looking like he was scared. Amanda had never seen this look before. He looked at her and said, "I have given you a fabulous life, and this is how you pay me back? I leave you for one night, and the next morning I find you in front of another hotel with a man holding his hand with two little boys. What was that all about?"

Amanda said, "I don't know, it seemed like I knew these two boys, but I can't make it all out." And then she began to yell at Dr. Collins, "You are sitting here asking me all these questions, but where were you last night?! Were you with another woman?"

"No! I was with some of the doctors that came to my conference. We were all talking and drinking and the time slipped away from me."

Amanda was looking at him as she said, "You made me your research, how could you do something like that? Your research is not all that, because you didn't know my dreams could wake up my memories. You built yourself up to be a powerful man, but in my books, you are nothing! One thing about life, you could not imagine anyone knowing me."

Dr. Collins looked at her and exploded. He began to knock everything over. Amanda began to scream for help. But there was no one there to help her.

Dr. Collins looked at her sharply and said, "You will never see our daughters again, and you will never walk beyond these doors. The only reason that you are still alive is because of my baby that you are carrying. I don't want anything to happen to our child that's inside of you." As he was walking out of the door, Amanda yelled, "Matthew, don't do this!"

Dr. Collins locked the door from the other side. He went down the stairs and called the butler back and told him to open the gates and let everyone back in. When everyone came back, he wanted to talk to the staff. He had one of his servants take his two daughters up to their room. Meanwhile, everyone else listened to what Dr. Collins had to say. While Dr. Collins was talking, one of his servants noticed that blood was on his shirt, but she didn't say anything. Dr. Collins told everyone that Amanda had left him, and that things were going to change. When he finished talking to everyone, he dismissed everyone except the butler and Miss Rose. Once they were alone, he said, "You are the only two people that I trust with my life and with everything I own. You have both been with me since the time I was born and I don't want anything but your loyalty." They said, "Yes, sir."

After the butler left the room, Miss Rose was given instructions to care for Amanda day by day. He told Miss Rose what happened and she took him in her arms and said, "I will take care of everything. Don't you worry."

Dr. Collins gave Miss Rose a key and said, "Please don't tell anyone and please keep everyone from that side of the mansion." Miss Rose gave him her word that she would be the only one to work on that side of the mansion.

Amanda had become very stressed out. She was in the room wondering about where she had come from, what was her real identity. All kinds of thoughts were going through her mind. One day, Beth and Angel were playing in the garden of flowers. Dr. Collins walked outside to where they were playing and, as he was calling them to him, he kept looking back up to the window of Amanda's room. By then she had cried herself to sleep. The girls wanted to know where their mother was. Dr. Collins said to them, "She had to go away on a business trip."

Beth said, "Dad, call her and tell her we miss her, we need her." He lied and said, "Okay, baby."

One of the servants overheard Beth talking to her father and she told the other servants, "Something is wrong. When have we ever known Mrs.

Collins to leave this mansion alone?" Miss Rose walked over to the maid and told her to get back to work.

Late that night, Amanda began to cry out for help, but no one heard her. Dr. Collins had a built-in camera in that room so he could watch her every move. He was the only one that could see her or hear her cries. Amanda finally got up and walked in front of the camera and said, "Matthew, I know that you are watching and listening to everything that I am doing! Matthew, please let me out of here! Please!"

Dr. Collins was in his room watching her and he also had it where she could see him in his room. His father had all those things put into the mansion when he tried to unsuccessfully kidnap his ex-wife. At least four times a day, Dr. Collins would lock himself into that room with Amanda. He would have Miss Rose change her bed coverings two times a week, and he would pick fresh flowers from his garden every day and bring them to her. One day Amanda tried to fight Dr. Collins and get past him but he put a needle in her arm to make her sleep for hours. When Amanda woke up, Miss Rose had cooked all of her favorite foods. Amanda didn't eat any of it. The next morning, Dr. Collins got up to ride one of his horses and Beth and Angel went running behind him.

They had begun fighting each other and they both cried out to him at one time. He was trying to understand what they were saying, so he called out to their handmaid so she could solve their problem but they both began to cry out for their mother. After he finished riding his horse, the girls were back playing with each other. Dr. Collins said, "Girls, I need for you two to come and walk with me." They ran to him and he told them that their mother had left them for another family and she didn't want them anymore.

Beth said, "Why did she leave us?"

He said, "She doesn't love us anymore, but I will never leave you."

Angel said, "She don't love us anymore?" "No!"

But they were strong about the news; they just looked up at him. When he walked back to the mansion, one of the servants said, "Dr. Collins, you have a very important call."

"Okay, take the girls."

When he reached the phone he found it was a lawyer for Antonio Jackson; they needed permission to come on his estate to find his wife.

Dr. Collins was surprised at first, then he got all the information and had his best friend, Jeff, handle everything for him.

Dr. Collins denied that he knew anything about a Vicki Jackson. Everything that Antonio and his attorneys tried to do, Dr. Collins would block them at every turn. Jeff told Dr. Collins not to worry about anything because they were out of their jurisdiction. Antonio just wanted to sit down with Dr. Collins to discuss the possibility that Mrs. Collins was his Vicki Jackson. Dr. Collins said, "No! There is no way that I'm letting you past my security. My wife and I have both agreed to separate and I do not know where she is. Mr. Jackson, please do not call my home again." As Dr. Collins was walking back to his seat, he really didn't know what to think. He picked up Amanda's pictures from off the table and said to himself out loud, "So that's who you are, Vicki Jackson." He told himself that he would never tell her, because "she will always be my Amanda Collins." The children were playing around and Dr. Collins called one of his handmaids to get the girls. After they left the room, Dr. Collins went into that room with Amanda. He wanted to talk to her, but Amanda would not talk with him.

He sat there for twenty minutes watching her. By now, Amanda was four months pregnant. He got ready to tell her who she was, but he decided not to. Amanda finally said, "Matthew, have the girls asked about me?" He looked at her and said, "Yes, and I have told them that you left us for another family."

"How are you going to pull this off? Are you going to keep the baby up here with me when it's born?"

Dr. Collins said, "I should check to see what sex my baby is." He had put everything he would need to deliver the baby in that room. As he was examining her, he found out that she was having a boy. Dr. Collins started laughing and said, "It's a boy! I'm having a son." But as soon as he walked out of the room, Amanda started hurting. Dr. Collins went back to his room, and was working on the Internet when he looked at the video screen and noticed that Amanda was lying on the floor and had blood on her clothes. He got his doctor's bag and rushed into the room to stop the bleeding. After he stopped the bleeding, he put her back onto her bed. Amanda kept having sharp pains in her stomach. She was so weak that he had Miss Rose stay with her while he went out.

One day while Dr. Collins was out, Amanda tried to talk Miss Rose into letting her go, but Miss Rose never answered her. Then Amanda said, "Miss Rose, how do you feel as a black woman watching another sister be treated like this? I'm locked away, and when I have this baby, he is not going to let me live. How will you feel when he kills me?" Miss Rose didn't say anything. She just stood up and walked out the door.

Two days later, Dr. Collins got a chair and he sat where he could see Amanda's window. For hours, he sat there under that tree. Everyone seemed to know that something was wrong. For a whole week, Dr. Collins wouldn't come into the mansion, he would be way in the back of his land digging this big hole in a field. One night when Miss Rose got ready to leave to go home, her car wouldn't start and the other servants had already left. Since there was no one in the mansion with the girls, Miss Rose decided to look for Dr. Collins after she had put the girls into bed. Miss Rose got ready to call out to him, but she noticed that he was digging a grave, so she took off running back into the mansion. When he returned to the mansion he said, "Miss Rose, I noticed that everyone has left but you."

She said, "Yes, my car wouldn't start."

He walked over to where he kept all of his keys for his cars and said, "Just take one of my cars." As Miss Rose was leaving,

Dr. Collins said, "Miss Rose, I need you to do something for me." "Whatever you need, Dr. Collins, I will do it for you,"

He said, "I know that I can depend on you. In the morning, I need you to be here early because my butler will be here at twelve o'clock noon. I have told the whole staff that they could be off, but I need you to be here by seven a.m. before I leave to go to the hospital. I have three new doctors coming in for interviews."

Miss Rose said, "I will be here early." Miss Rose got into one of Dr. Collins cars and she left. She was so scared going down that road that she didn't know what to do.

The next morning, Miss Rose arrived early. As Dr. Collins was walking out the door, Miss Rose was pulling up. He kissed Miss Rose on her head as he said, "Listen, when the butler comes in, please call me. The girls are still asleep. Please check on my wife."

"Yes, sir, but how long will you be gone, Dr. Collins?"

"I should be here no later than one o'clock this afternoon."

When Miss Rose went into the mansion, she made sure that everything was clear. Miss Rose got on the phone and called her son, because Dr. Collins didn't know that Miss Rose had a son. Miss Rose told her son, "Listen, Dr. Collins is not here, and by the time you get here, I will make sure that everyone is ready to leave. So bring that package with all of that information in it, we don't have no time to lose."

Miss Rose went into Dr. Collins' room and opened his safe and got over forty thousand dollars in cash out for Amanda. Then she packed some of the girls' clothes and some of Amanda's clothes. When her son arrived, Amanda had gotten up and she noticed that this car was rushing into the driveway. She saw this man get out of his car and Miss Rose run out to meet him. Then she noticed that he put both of her daughters into that car while they were both still asleep. She began to scream, "No, No!!" But then Miss Rose unlocked the door and she said, "Hurry up, honey, and let's get out of here."

As Amanda was going to the car, Miss Rose said, "Goodbye, Mrs. Vicki Jackson." Amanda looked at Miss Rose and didn't understand why she called her Vicki Jackson, but she got into the car and they headed for North Carolina. The young man handed Amanda a package with everything in it. As she was reading the information, she began to cry with tears of joy. The driver's cell phone rang and it was Mr. Smith. "Did you get my daughter and my grandbabies?"

The driver said, "Yes sir, let me give her the phone." Amanda began to yell out, "Is this my dad?"

Mr. Smith cried, "Yes, baby, how are you?" "I'm okay now."

"You know your name is not Amanda, your name is Vicki Smith Jackson."

Vicki took her name back that very hour. Mrs. Smith was lying in the next room from her husband when she overheard what he had said. Mrs. Smith reached for the phone, she tried to talk but she couldn't utter more than, "Vi —, Vi—"

Vicki said, "Mom, what is wrong with your voice?"

Mr. Smith took the phone back from his wife and said, "Baby, we will talk about everything when you get here. You will not be coming right here to the house, though. I have another home ready for you because when that crazy man finds out that you are not there, this will be the first place that he will look. When you get to this secret home, baby, we will be right here, so Vicki, get some rest." Vicki and the girls had been on the road for four hours and thirty minutes. Finally, the driver had to stop to fuel up again, and Vicki told him to please hurry.

It was getting close to twelve o'clock and the butler was on his way to the mansion. As the butler was arriving, he noticed that the gate was open. He got out of his car and ran up the steps of the mansion yelling out, "Who left the gate open?" But no one answered him because no one was there. All the doors were open. He rushed over to the phone to call Dr. Collins. When the hospital paged Dr. Collins, the butler told him that he needed to get home because something was wrong. Dr. Collins asked him, "What is going on?"

"I found the gate open and no one is here, not even your wife and children." Dr. Collins yelled out, "What?! I will be home as soon as possible."

When Dr. Collins arrived at the mansion, he ran straight to his children's room and saw they were not there, then he ran into his wife's room and saw she was gone. Dr. Collins began weeping uncontrollably. Then he became very angry and violent and started knocking over everything. He fell down in this chair. Then he picked up the phone and called a very good friend of his, a Frenchman by the name of Mike. He told Mike to bring him a gun, and Mike said, "I'm on my way." Dr. Collins began to cry.

When Mike arrived, he went into the mansion and stood directly in front of Dr. Collins. That's when Dr. Collins told the butler to leave because he didn't know whom to trust. When the butler left, Dr.

Collins turned to the Frenchman and said, "Do you have the gun?" Mike handed it to him. Dr.

Collins stood up and said, "Mike, when we were young men, I helped you and your family come to this country, and my father made sure that your parents had a home and a good job. What I really need to know is, are you loyal to me?"

Mike said, "Yes I am.

"I need you to show your devotion to me once again."

"Whatever you need, I'm the man for the job." Dr. Collins said, "I need you to help me clean up something before I leave town, and I need you to be my driver all the way."

Dr. Collins had the Frenchman drive him to Miss Rose's home. They waited until it was dark to go there. When they first arrived, Miss Rose was not there, but it wasn't long before she came driving up. As she was getting out of the car, Dr. Collins pulled up right behind her. Mike put a gun to her head and he said with a heavy voice, "Miss Rose, get into my car." Miss Rose was so scared as she was walking back to his car that she was shaking.

When he opened the door of the car, Miss Rose sat down right beside Dr. Collins. She looked at him and she said, "Oh, it's you, what's going on, Dr. Collins?"

He didn't say anything at first but just looked at her.

Then he said, "How could you do this to me, Miss Rose?"

She could tell that he had been crying, and she tried to comfort him but he moved her hand away from him. Mike drove them back to the mansion.

When they got her to the mansion, Dr. Collins said, "Have a seat, Miss Rose. I just want you to watch television with me." Then he said, "You know better than anyone that everything that goes on around here gets recorded." He turned the television on and put a tape into the VCR to show her what the camera caught. As she was looking at the video, he stood over her. "Miss Rose." Dr. Collins said, "I'm so sorry. I have been with you since the day that I was born. Just think how much I love you and even looked up to you as a mother. I gave you everything, and this is how you repay me?"

Miss Rose said, "Please, Dr. Collins, let me explain why I did what I did." She was trying to plead her case. Dr. Collins told Mike, "Just take her out of here!" Miss Rose began to call out to the butler, but Dr. Collins said, "Oh, he can't help you, he has the night off." The Frenchman just pulled her up from the chair and carried her outside. She yelled for help while he was dragging her to the hole that Dr. Collins had dug for Amanda.

When Miss Rose realized that this man was going to kill her, she looked up towards heaven and she said these words: "No weapon that's formed against me shall prosper, It won't work. God will come through for me." Then she began to repeat Psalm 23 verse 4.

"Yea, though I walk through the valley of the shadow of death, I will fear no evil: for thou art with me, thy rod and thy staff, they comfort me." When she finished saying that, she looked the Frenchman in his eyes and he shot her three times. Then he laid her in the grave and covered her up.

Meanwhile, Dr. Collins was still looking at the video, and he saw one of his handmaids hitting one of his daughters. He got up from his chair, called all of them, and fired every one of them. By now, the whole staff was hurt, because they have lost their jobs. When the Frenchman came back into the room with Dr. Collins, he lied and said, "She tried to escape, I had no choice. It's done." Then Dr. Collins called Jeff to come over. When Jeff arrived, he told him everything – except that Miss Rose was dead. Jeff said, "Let's get ready to go to North Carolina."

They had the pilot get the jet ready. Jeff handed Dr. Collins some more information about his wife, but he already knew that Amanda was really Vicki Jackson, a famous author, and that her husband had made himself a millionaire, and that they had two little boys. Jeff said, "Matthew, from the look on your face, you already know about this. Dr. Collins said, "Jeff, I don't care about who she's supposed to be. All I know is that she has my two daughters with her and she is pregnant with my son. And I want them back." Jeff said, "Okay, no one can deny you your children, but let's do this thing the right way. We can get a court order for you to take the girls back and, when the baby is born, we can take her to court and get your son."

"No, Jeff, these people are powerful and it would be dragged out in the courts for a long time. It would bring the media in and they would have it all over the news. I don't want her to get her memory back right now, because if she does, she will run back into Antonio's arms, and I will not have her running right along with my children. That's my father's blood line! I can't let her live a day after she has my son! Because if I can't have her, then no one will."

Jeff just stood and looked at him and he was looking at Jeff as if he was ready for battle. Dr. Collins told his pilot to get ready to fly to North Carolina. Dr. Collins said, "Jeff, are you the only one loyal to me?"

"Yes," Jeff said, and then the pilot arrived and they boarded the jet to North Carolina.

After they arrive in North Carolina, they went looking for both Mr. Smith's and Antonio's homes. Mr. Smith alerted Antonio as to what to look out for, so Antonio would be ready for Dr. Collins. Mr. Smith told Antonio not to get hot-headed because he needed to protect the boys as well. He also told him that he had Vicki and her daughters in hiding until this danger passes them by.

Antonio said, "Does she remember anything about me?"

"No," Mr. Smith said, then added, "I have made it so Vicki won't have to come outside."

"I want to see her, and what do I tell my boys?"

Mr. Smith said, "Nothing right now, because the least that they know, the safer they are."

"They know that their mother is alive."

Mr. Smith said, "Antonio, you are a very smart young man, so handle your part the best you can and be careful. I'm not planning on losing any of my grandbabies because of the wrong steps that we make, son. Dr. Collins is a very deadly man!"

As they were talking, a knock came at Antonio's door. Antonio said, "Hold on, Dad." When he went to the door, it was Dr. Collins, Jeff, and the Frenchman. They just walked in and started looking around. Antonio said, "You must be Dr. Collins. I don't remember asking you to come in."

Dr. Collins walked up close to Antonio and said, "Where are my wife and my girls?"

"I don't know what you are talking about."

When Antonio said that, Dr. Collins tried to fight. Meanwhile, Jeff and Mike began to check Antonio's home. When he pushed Antonio, Antonio came back at him, but Dr. Collins put his hand on his gun as if he were going to pull it out. And then he said to Antonio, "Make my day." Then Jeff and Mike walked back into the room and they said, "She is not here."

As they were walking out of his house, Antonio said, "Man, you better not ever walk back into my home again." Dr. Collins gave him an evil look.

Antonio got back on the phone with his father-in-law and said, "Did you hear them?"

"Yes, son, and you better believe that they are not going anywhere any time soon. Antonio, we are going to have to be careful about our phone calls, because they could tap our phones, so be very, very careful, this may be a good time to talk to your mother and father. Maybe your mom can get the boys away for a while."

"That would be a good idea." As Antonio was looking out the window, that black car was still sitting there. Antonio could see that they were reading a map, and then they pulled off. He saw them as they turned the corner going towards Mr. Smith's home. Antonio was still on the phone with Mr. Smith, so he said, "Dad, it looks like you are getting ready to receive some company."

Mr. Smith said, "I'm ready for them."

As Antonio was hanging up the phone, he decided to walk over to his mother and father's home which was across the street from the Smiths' home. By this time, Dr. Collins had made it to Mr. Smith's home, and he and the other two men were walking up to the door. Mr. Smith didn't give them time to knock, he just opened the door and stood in their way. "What do you want, Dr. Collins?"

Dr. Collins looked around, then at Mr. Smith and he said, "Is this any way to treat your new son-in-law, Dad?"

"You are not my son-in-law!"

Dr. Collins said, "Let's cut all of the small talk, you know why I'm here. Where's your daughter, Mr. Smith? She has something of mine and I want it back." Dr. Collins was getting angry and he and his men pushed their way into the house. By now, Antonio had reached his parents' home and then called the police. When the police arrived, Dr. Collins and his men were already checking Mr. Smith's home, so Mr. Smith yelled out, "Officers, these men pushed their way into my home, they are trespassing."

The officer looked at everyone and said, "First of all, I'm going to have to see some I.D. from everybody." When Jeff showed his I.D. and the officer saw that Jeff worked as a lawyer for the government, he asked Mr. Smith to step back into his home then asked the others to step back into their car so he could talk to Jeff. When Dr. Collins and the Frenchman got back into the car, they hid their guns under their seat so the policeman couldn't see them. Jeff told the officer that someone had broken into his client's home and stole over forty thousand dollars from him. He added that they kidnapped Dr. Matthew Collins' wife and children. The officer said, "The surgeon that is known all over the world?"

Jeff said, "Yes."

Then the officer said, "I don't mean any harm, but what do these people have to do with it?"

"We came here looking for Mrs. Collins because she is very sick and she is pregnant. Plus, this is her parents' home, and we have reason to believe that her parents are hiding her along with Dr. Collins' children. My client is worried out of his mind."

The officer said, "I understand." Then he asked Jeff to wait in his car until he talked to Mr. Smith. As the officer was walking back toward Mr. Smith he said, "Do you know where your daughter is?"

Mr. Smith said, "Let me talk to you."

The officer barked, "Just answer my question!" "No!"

The officer said, "Mr. Smith, it's against the law to kidnap this man's family." Then he walked to the car where Jeff was sitting and he told him to follow him back to the police station to file a missing person's report on Mrs. Collins and her children. Mr. Smith yelled out to the officer, "No matter how far we have come, or what we have accomplished, it still goes back to there is no justice in this world for us." The officer drove off holding his head high as if he didn't hear him. After everyone left, Mr.

Smith walked across the street to where Mr. and Mrs. Jackson and Antonio were standing. He said, "I know that you already have heard that my daughter is still alive, but as you can see, the law is not on our side, and that's why I'm going to have to keep her in hiding.

These people will take my grandbabies away from me. And after she has the baby that she is carrying, they will kill her." Then all he could do was cry.

Antonio said, "Did you say that Vicki is pregnant?"

"Yes, that's all the man did was keep her pregnant. He wouldn't let her have her tubes tied. Vicki told us everything."

Antonio looked at his mom and dad, and then Mrs. Jackson said, "What can we do to help?"

Mr. Smith replied, "Get our grandchildren out of here for at least two months until things calm down."

Mr. Jackson said, "I agree, because they are home schooled anyway, and we need to keep them safe." As Mrs. Jackson was getting ready to pack up some clothes, Mr. Jackson said to her, "Honey, you don't have any time to pack, just redo your closet when you get to your aunt's house. I really need you to go and pick up the grandchildren while Dr. Collins and his men are still at the police station."

As he was kissing Mrs. Jackson before she left, Antonio said, "Mom, please drive carefully and tell my sons I love them. I know that Auntie will be glad to see you and the boys and, whatever you do, don't call the house phone.

We will get in touch with you."

Mr. Smith said, "My wife is already gone, she left after she met with Vicki. Bella is staying with her sister in another town." Mrs. Jackson started crying as she was leaving. Mrs. Jackson drove to the baby sitter's house, and when Antonio Jr. and Ja'cob ran out to the car, they were so happy to see their grandma. When they got into the car. Mrs. Jackson said,

"Boys, we are going to take a little trip, somewhere out of the state." Antonio Jr. said, "Does Dad know?"

"Yes."

The boys said, "Does it have anything to do with our mom?" "I didn't know that you knew anything about that."

Ja'cob said, "We saw her in New York one time, but she really didn't know who our dad was."

Mrs. Jackson said, "Well, he's trying to get her to remember everyone." The boys were so happy about it that they didn't say anything else.

Mrs. Jackson drove for three hours to West Virginia, in the beautiful west side, where her aunt was expecting them. Meanwhile, Dr. Collins and his men stayed in town for nearly three weeks. The police put out a missing person's report for Amanda Collins, who was going by the name of Vicki Smith Jackson. Dr. Collins put out a reward for two hundred thousand dollars leading to information on their whereabouts.

They profiled Vicki, Beth, and Angel. Their pictures were all over the news, and, because of who Dr. Collins was, the news went international. Jeff told everyone to stay calm and let the police do their job, and then he told Dr.

Collins that he had to go back to California because one of his cases was coming up and he had to prepare for it. Jeff said, "Matthew, it's getting close to time for Vicki to have her baby, so why don't we all just go back home and wait until she goes into labor?"

Dr. Collins looked at Jeff, and said, "I don't know any Vicki,

I named her Amanda." Jeff said, "The officer that helped us, why don't you secretly put him on your payroll and we can get updates from him on the Internet every day? She can't stay in hiding forever.

Once she comes out and checks into the hospital, we will be right back here to get your sons and your two daughters. We will be on her so fast, she won't know what's going on, and right now we have the upper hand in all of this."

Jeff called the officer over to their hotel and, when he got there, Dr. Collins made him an offer that he couldn't refuse. He put a suitcase on the table with fifty thousand dollars in cash in it. Dr. Collins said, "All I want you to be is my eyes and ears, because I don't just trust everyone, and there's more money from where this came from. I had you checked out, I know you are about to lose your home, so I can help you."

The officer looked at the money and said, "Dr. Collins, is that all I have to do? Just to be your eyes and ears?" As the officer was counting the money, Dr. Collins said, "I believe in loyalty and no less than that." The officer assured him, "I will be nothing but loyal to you," and he took the money and left.

Dr. Collins, Jeff, and the Frenchman went back to California. Every day the officer sat in front of Mr. Jackson's home and Mr. Smith's home.

He watched all of them, but as weeks went by, the officer was put on another duty which took him away from the Jackson and Smith homes. It wasn't long before Vicki went into labor. She had an eight-pound boy. While she was in the hospital, one of the nurses saw her chart and called the 1-800 number Dr. Collins had posted. When he got the call, the nurse asked him if he was still paying two hundred thousand dollars for information on his wife's whereabouts.

He said, "Yes!"

Then she said, "I could really get in a lot of trouble for doing this."

"Please, don't worry about it, no one will know that you have spoken to me. Please tell me where she is."

The nurse said, "Will you have my money when you arrive?" "Every penny of it."

After the nurse gave him the information that he needed, he called Jeff, and the Frenchman. After they arrived at the mansion, Dr. Collins called his pilot to fuel up the jet.

When everyone boarded the jet, Jeff looked at Dr. Collins and said, "Matthew, I need you to stay in control, and whatever you do, don't lose it."

Dr. Collins said, "What do you mean? I'm a businessman, and I own an empire, so what do you mean about staying in control?" His whole personality had changed. Jeff kept watching him, and when they arrived in North Carolina, they went straight to the hospital. But they were thirty minutes too late, Vicki had been discharged. When the nurse saw him, she pulled him to the side because she didn't want anyone to overhear her. She said, "I'm so sorry, but she's gone. However, I do have something for you. I have her address, phone number, and a copy of the boy's birth certificate.

And I did take some pictures for you while he was in the nursery."

As he was looking at the pictures of his son and the birth certificate, he asked the nurse, "Why didn't you call earlier?" The nurse said, "Well, I have been off of work sick, and this is my first day back." Dr. Collins took out his checkbook and wrote her a ten thousand dollar check. She looked at it and said, "This is not what we agreed to."

Dr. Collins replied, "We agreed that you would give me my family, but I don't see anyone standing here but us four."

As they were walking away, Jeff was looking at the baby picture and said, "Little Jr. looks just like your father."

Dr. Collins exploded, "When I get my hands on her, she will die very slowly, and I am going to be there to watch it! I have got to get my son and my daughters."

While Dr. Collins was talking, Jeff looked at the address and said, "This is not your wife's address, this is her father's address and phone number."

Dr. Collins said, "Let me see that. Well, this is not where she lives, but let's drive by there anyway."

Then the Frenchman said, "Dr. Collins, what happened to the officer that you hired to keep a watch out for you?" Dr. Collins said, "That's a good question. Well, I'm just going to have to wait her out. I'm not going back to California until I find my children."

The Frenchman said, "I need to put a tap on her parents' and her in-laws' phones."

Dr. Collins said, "Why didn't we think of that anyway?"

After Vicki had her baby, she stayed in hiding, but one day the girls wanted to go outside to play. They were so tired of being inside the house, and Vicki had already told them about their other brothers and they wanted to meet them. So Vicki thought it would be safe to go out, since she hadn't heard anything about Matthew. She called Antonio, not knowing that his phone was tapped and that Dr. Collins was back in town. Vicki talked to Little Ja'cob and Antonio Jr. and then she let the girls talk to their brothers. They stayed on the phone for so long that Dr. Collins was able to trace the call and get her real address. He heard Vicki's plans to meet with Antonio and her boys at the park.

Antonio said to Vicki, "I miss you and you just don't know how much I love you."

Vicki said, "We have so much to talk about. And the girls are so excited to meet their brothers."

Antonio said, "Do you remember the park in front of our home? Well, let's meet there at two o'clock this afternoon." Vicki agreed. When they finished talking, they didn't even think that the phone had been tapped. Dr. Collins had heard every word they said.

Jeff said, "Well, she just made her first mistake."

Dr. Collins said, "No, she did that when she took my children away from me."

It was getting close to two o'clock, and all three of them had left the hotel in order to get there first. They parked across the street, where Vicki couldn't see them. They were riding in a black BMW with tinted windows, and all of them had sunglasses on. It wasn't long before Antonio arrived with his boys. He was looking around to make sure that it was safe. The boys began to run around the park, and Antonio got on the phone and called Vicki. She asked him if it was safe to come, and he said yes. Dr. Collins heard that too.

Dr. Collins looked at Jeff and said, "Jeff, you and I have been friends for too long to let a woman come between us, so whatever happens today, the main thing is to get my children out of here safely. Okay? Does everyone understand?" They both said yes.

While they were talking, Vicki arrived with the two girls running in front of her. She was carrying the baby in his little car seat as she walked towards Antonio. They greeted each other with a hug, Antonio began to cry and said, "You are so beautiful," and Vicki just smiled. Antonio took the baby while Vicki was getting the baby's bag out of the car. Dr. Collins and his men were watching them, and he said, "What does she think she's doing, handing my son to Antonio?" He took out his gun becasue he wanted to shoot both of them right there, while Vicki and Antonio were sitting and talking.

But two police cars pulled up, and when they got out of their cars to talk, Dr. Collins put his gun away. The girls took off running with their newfound brothers, but Vicki yelled out to them to come over to her because she wanted to see Antonio Jr. and Little Ja'cob.

The boys ran up to Vicki and they said, "Are you, our mom?" Vicki laughed out loud and said, "Yes I am," and she bent down to hug and kiss them. Beth and Angel joined in, Vicki began to cry, and the boys wanted to know if she was glad to see them. Vicki said, "I am so happy." Beth said, "Don't worry about Mom, she is always crying." They were so loud that they woke up baby Matthew, and he began to cry, and when Antonio picked him up from his car seat and gave him the bottle.

Dr. Collins was at the edge of his seat, he was so mad. Then he got out of the car, but Vicki did not see him. Vicki and Antonio started talking again, the children were having so much fun. Antonio began to rock little Matthew back to sleep. Then he handed the baby back to Vicki and she laid him in his car seat right beside her. Antonio looked at Vicki and he said, "Vicki, I want you back in my life."

"Antonio," she said, "I understand what you are feeling, but you are going to have to give me some time. I don't need to rush into a relationship with you or anyone else now. That wouldn't be fair to your feelings, not when I don't even know myself."

Antonio said, "Baby, I've never stopped loving you. Why don't you give us a chance?"

She said, "Things have really changed for me. I have three more children that belong to someone else. And I have to think about them."

"Vicki, you are still my wife and I'm not going to let you go. And if you give me a chance, I will be a good father to all of your children. I will try my very best to keep you happy. One thing that I have never done was put my hands on you or make you cry. Vicki, I have something that I want you to hear." Antonio took this big boom box and he played one of their wedding songs. The name of the song was "Superstar/Until You Come Back to Me" by Luther Vandross. Antonio stood up in front of Vicki and he said, "May I have this dance?" As he was pulling her to him, they began to slow dance with each other. At that very moment, Antonio kissed her very passionately on the mouth. Vicki kissed him back. Antonio whispered in Vicki's ear and said, "Baby, I love you." Vicki was in Antonio's arms. As he was kissing her down her neck, Beth fell and cried out for her mother. Vicki heard Beth crying and took off running towards her.

Dr. Collins was looking at everything. He began to run to help Beth but Jeff stopped him. Vicki noticed that Beth's leg was bleeding. She put a band-aid on it. Then she told her boys, "We will be together soon, but right now I have to go, so give me a hug."

The boys hugged and kissed their mother goodbye. She looked at Antonio with tears in her eyes and said, "This is not the time. We will talk soon."

Antonio helped Vicki to get the children into the car and then he looked at her and said, "I love you, let's not wait too long." She didn't say anything. Antonio went back to play with his boys as Vicki was leaving. As she drove to her secret home, she never looked back to see that Dr. Collins was following her. As she arrived, the girls jumped out of the car and ran to the door. Vicki was getting little Matthew's car seat out of the car. As she took it into the house, her phone was ringing. When she reached the phone, she found out it was her father. He asked her, "Where have you been all day?"

"Dad, hold on for a minute," she put the baby down and yelled upstairs to Beth and Angel to wash their hands and get ready for dinner.

Vicki went back to get the phone. She said, "Dad, I'm back." as she was walking towards the door to close it. As she was closing it, Dr. Collins put his foot inside the door to block her. As he was pushing his way in, Vicki yelled out, "Dad, please call the police, Matthew is here!" Then she screamed to the girls, "Girls run to your room and lock the door!"

She was trying to get away from him, and the girls heard their mother screaming for help. Dr. Collins knocked the phone out of Vicki's hand then took his fist and hit Vicki in the face, knocking her onto the floor. Vicki was fighting back but she was losing. He was beating her so badly that Vicki couldn't get away from him. He yelled out, "I saw you in the park today! I saw everything! How could you kiss Antonio in front of my babies!?! And you let him hold my son, and you danced with this man!!!"

He had no mercy on her as he was beating her. He hit her so hard that her head hit the wall and she was knocked unconscious. As she was laying there bleeding, Dr. Collins began to choke her. He said, "Congratulations, you have just signed your death warrant!" Then he took out a gun, put it to her head, and said, "Goodbye, Amanda."

Jeff ran into the house to tell him to stop because the police were on their way. But he just kept on beating her. So, Jeff and the Frenchman got out of there. By now, the baby was crying and the girls were crying out upstairs. Dr. Collins got ready to remove the safety off of the gun, and the police ran into the house with their guns drawn. Mr. Smith and Antonio were right behind the officers. The police demanded that Dr. Collins drop his gun.

They told him, "If you don't drop that gun, you will force us to shoot you!"

Mr. Smith said, "Dr. Collins, don't kill my only daughter. Just please son, don't do it."

Dr. Collins yelled, "I'm not your son!"

That's when Beth and Angel ran downstairs and yelled, "Dad, NO!! Please Dad, don't kill our mom!"

The police yelled out, "Take these children out of here!" Dr. Collins looked up at his daughters and cried out, "My babies!"

Angel ran over to her father and he dropped the gun. Vicki was unconscious.

They called an ambulance to take her to the hospital. Dr. Collins was arrested and taken to jail for the attempted murder of his wife. Dr. Collins was trying to get out on bond, but the judge denied him a bond at that time. The judge sent word to Dr. Collins that he wasn't getting out of jail until the courts made sense of what was going on.

Vicki was in the hospital for two days. Antonio took all of the children to his parents' home. Everyone was so worried about Vicki's situation. Mr. and Mrs. Jackson made room for Beth, Angel, little Mathew, Antonio Jr., and Little Ja'cob. Mr. Smith and Antonio stayed at the hospital with Vicki. They would not leave her side. The same day that Vicki was released from the hospital, the judge called a very important meeting with Vicki, Antonio, and Dr. Collins and their attorneys. He wanted to meet with everyone in the courthouse conference room to discuss their problem. Antonio called his brother Ja'cob in New York. He said, "Ja'cob, how long would it take you to fly out to North Carolina today?"

Ja'cob said, "What is it that you need?"

"The superior court judge is calling for an emergency meeting between myself, Vicki, and Dr. Collins."

Ja'cob said, "I'm taking the next flight out. I will be there soon."

Vicki was at her parents' house when she received the call that the judge wanted to meet with everyone. She could barely walk and had dark bruises all over her face, neck, and arms. She was laying down when the call came. Antonio also called her. She asked Antonio if the children were okay, and he said yes. She said, "Antonio, I don't want my children to see me looking like this."

Antonio said, "Don't worry about anything, we are taking care of the children. One more thing, Ja'cob is on his way and he will be representing you and me."

Vicki said, "Do you think that he will get here on time?"

"He is going straight to the courthouse." Then, as he was hanging up the phone, Antonio said, "Vicki, I love you." But she didn't say it back. She just hung up.

Dr. Collins called Jeff from the county jail and told him about the meeting. Jeff was still in town with the Frenchman. Jeff said, "I will be right over."

When everyone arrived at the meeting, a sheriff was standing in front of the door to escort them to the conference room. Everyone was told to sit down at a big table. Dr. Collins walked in with a guard beside him and shackles around his feet. The expression on his face was very tense as he spoke with his lawyer, Jeff.

Antonio sat right beside Vicki, and she sat across the table from Dr. Collins. By now, Ja'cob had arrived. The meeting had not started yet. Several unsure thoughts crossed Vicki's mind as she was sitting at the table with Antonio and Dr. Collins and their lawyers. When the door began to open, she saw that it was the judge. The tall man wearing a black robe seemed to know exactly what he was coming to do. He put on his glasses as he opened a file. He made several different facial expressions as he read. "Mrs. Jackson, is it?" The judge asked. "Yes," she responded in an assertive voice.

"From what I understand, you are married to one Antonio Jackson?" "Yes, sir." She responded, trying to keep her voice from cracking. The judge said, "I understand you are also married to one Dr. Matthew Collins."

He sounded as if he knew this would be a long day coming.

"In this proceeding, I want all three of you to explain to me exactly what is going on." He looked at Dr. Collins and said, "Right now, you are in the custody of the county jail without bond. And you also have a temporary restraining order against you by Mrs. Vicki Jackson for trying to take the three children away from her that the both of you share and also for trying to kill her." He continued, "I will be making my ruling when I hear from everyone, and I'm going to start with Mrs. Vicki Jackson. Mrs. Jackson, you will be able to speak to each of these men. You can start whenever you please."

Vicki said, "Antonio, let me say something to you first. It has come to my attention that, before my plane accident, we were high school sweethearts and we married each other with so much love. And the things that I have heard about you are heart-warming. I have tried so hard to remember you, but I can't. I'm so sorry about the kiss in the park the other day. I feel that, as a result of my recovery, I just can't lead you on, you are too nice of a guy for that, and you deserve better than that. But thank you for agreeing to share custody of the children with me.

But I would like to change some things, instead of home schooling, I would like to see them in classes with their own peers. I really feel that they would build their character better knowing that they are just as good as the next person." The judge looked at her as she was talking and he began to write down something. He was also looking at Antonio's and Dr. Collins' reactions.

Vicki went on, "I won't hold you to your promise in marriage because I don't remember it. Whenever you want to file for divorce, please just let me know because, by law, you are my legal husband."

Then Vicki turned to Dr. Collins to say something, and began to cry out, "Ohhh, ohhh, Matthew!" Everything became so silent. The judge stopped writing and he had a very unsettled look on his face as he eyed Dr. Collins. Vicki was trying to find the words to say. She said, "Matthew, you are the man that I know, and still I love you. But I am so much afraid of you. Matthew, you were like my morning light, when the sun rises without a cloud in the sky. And I felt as if I was the tender grass springing out of the earth beneath you after the rain."

"Matthew," she continued while looking at him steadily, "you may have broken my spirit, but I am healed. When we first got together, your words were smoother than butter. And when you poured that soft oil all over me, you had my whole heart, mind, body, and soul. And then one day you changed, and for some reason, I became your worst enemy. You came after me with full hatred, ready for battle. You locked me away, and that is something that I will never forget, and the beating!!! I will never let you or any man hit me again. I am complete, but no man completed me. I may have some of my memory gone, but I am here, so I thank God for what I have. Matthew, you always talk about loyalty to you, but what about loyalty to me?" Vicki finished talking, and looked down, where tears just ran down her face.

The judge said, "Dr. Collins, I need you to respond to what Mrs. Jackson just said."

Dr. Collins looked at Vicki and his eyes seemed to give a perception of why he was so angry, and he said, "Vicki, I am so sorry about the way that I have treated you, please forgive me. Vicki, teach me how to love you, because I can't live one moment without you. And teach me how to be true to you and our children. I love you."

The judge looked up and he said, "Mr. Antonio Jackson, talk to us."

Antonio said, "First of all, this has saddened me. I never thought in a million years that life could turn upside down like this. I feel so guilty that I wasn't there for my wife when she needed me the most. But when flight 417 went down and the UFC's said that there were no survivors, my life was destroyed. For many years, I tried to do the right thing by watching over our sons, Antonio, Jr. and Ja'cob. I tried to be a good father, and Vicki, I tried to keep your dream alive with your children's books, putting them out there in the world for all the children to read. But what kept me going is your love, the love that we shared as one. I can't really describe in detail how I feel right now. Listening to you tell another man how much you love him and, at the same time, you really don't even know me. I have never locked you away. I have never hit you. I have always let you have your way about everything. Even the day that you wanted to go to California, I didn't have a good feeling about it. But you cried to your mother and I gave in, and now you have three other children and you're married to a man that is heartless.

What do you want me to say? That this is okay because you lost your memory? I don't know what to say. This hurts so bad. You don't love me, you love him. But even if you take Dr. Collins back, I don't want any fighting around my boys and I don't want them to leave town with anyone. Yes, I have agreed to share custody with you, but I want my boys in a safe environment. Vicki, I am not going to make the call on the divorce.

Whenever you are ready to make that call, you let me know, and I will sign the papers. But I have decided to move out of the house because you need the room with five children. I will not stay in a place with you when you don't even know me. But when I want to see my boys, I will call you first to let you know that I'm picking them up," he said with some what anger in his voice. He continued, "I also have some bank statements that belong to you from the sale of your books." When he handed them to her and she saw that her books had made her many thousands of dollars, she couldn't believe her eyes. Antonio began to cry.

The judge said, "I'm ready to make my ruling in this matter." He looked down at his notes and said, "Dr. Collins, considering the way that you have been aggressive, obsessive and very abusive toward, and even threatened Mrs. Vicki Jackson, I'm keeping the temporary restraining order against you. And you will have supervisory visitations with your three children by Mrs. Jackson. And I will also order you to participate in a program for battered women and, for the next four months, you are hereby ordered to go to a retreat for anger management. And you will not threaten or hit Mrs.

Jackson again." He told the jailer to release Dr. Collins and said, "You better not go anywhere near her in any way. If you do, you will be spending time in jail. Dr. Collins, you have an obligation to take care of your children, and so do you, Mr. Antonio Jackson." Both men said, "Yes, sir," at the same time. Then the judge said, "Mrs. Jackson, I understand that you have been through a lot and you have come a mighty long way. But you are a brave woman. And I also understand that you wish to continue sharing custody with Mr. Jackson of your two boys." Vicki said, "Yes, sir."

The judge said, "I have no other choice but to allow Dr. Matthew Collins to share custody of his three children with you when he finishes what was ordered by the courts. I find no deception in this case because, Mrs. Jackson, you were in a plane crash and your seat was ejected from the plane and you landed on the property where Dr. Collins did find you, and he saved you. Even before he knew who you were, you both fell in love with each other. He paid your hospital bills. The courts understand that the accident caused you to lose your memory. And Mr. Jackson, my heart goes out to you, this has got to be hard on you. But I look at it this way, your children will have a good mother and all five children will have a chance to learn from her. Mr. Jackson, I am going to leave it up to you and your wife, Mrs. Vicki Jackson, to work out your visitations and whether you will be paying her for child support for the two children. Mr. Jackson, I don't need to see you again. However, if you decide that you want your divorce, just get the papers prepared and I will sign them. And Dr. Collins, I want you to start right away on what the court has ordered you to do, and after you finish with everything, I will need for you and Mrs. Jackson to come back before this court."

The judge sighed heavily and concluded, "Dr. Collins and Mrs. Jackson, your marriage is not validated in this court. I feel like everyone has been completely honest and accurate in this meeting. I feel that every one of you need to work on your relationships for the children's sake. And I'm putting a seal on this meeting. None of you is allowed to talk about what went on in here to anyone. I don't feel that you want the news media to sit out in front of your home every day, because that wouldn't be good for the children.

Your obligation is to the children." The judge looked at Vicki and he said, "I'm going to allow you to have the last words."

Vicki said, "I'm a stranger to myself. Please, Matthew and Antonio, allow me to learn who I am. It would be wrong for me to lead the both of you on, so I'm not asking either one of you to wait for me. But the one thing that I do know is that I am the mother of Antonio, Jr., Ja'cob, Beth, Angel, and Matthew, Jr., and no other woman is going to take my place with my children. And before you come to visit with the children, please call to let me know. And I will be moving back into my home."

Antonio and Dr. Collins and their lawyers were walking out of the meeting while looking back at Vicki as she looked over her papers. They were sad, but she was so happy. The judge looked at her and said, "Welcome back, Mrs. Jackson." Ja'cob looked at Antonio and said, "Dr. Collins got off easy, and brother, if I were you, I would be preparing those divorce papers.

Later, Jeff took Dr. Collins to the retreat to begin his community service. Jeff asked him, "Don't you think that Vicki acted a little strange after the meeting was over?" Dr. Collins said, "No, that's my wife and I love her with my whole heart, and I'm going to fight for her." As they were talking, Dr. Collins took out his checkbook and wrote Vicki a check for nearly seventy million dollars. Then he also wrote her a letter promising her that he was going to get the help that he needed. He wanted her to wait for him. And he reminded her that she still had the mansion in London. He put the check and the letter in an envelope and told Jeff to take it to Vicki as soon as he dropped him off. By now, Vicki had gone back to her mother and father's house. Mrs. Jackson still had all of the children.

Antonio and Ja'cob had gone back to Antonio's house to start packing his things. Ja'cob said to Antonio, "This was about the strangest meeting that I have ever been in, the judge did not allow the lawyers to speak." Antonio was mad. But he kept on packing. He left the boys' things there. Vicki's clothes were still in the same place that she had left them before the plane wreck. After Antonio moved back into his parents' house to be close to where his boys lived, Vicki moved into his house with all five of her children. A few weeks later, Jeff came by her home and gave her the letter. As she was reading it, she noticed the check. She didn't know what to say. She took the check to the bank and deposited it. Every weekend, Antonio would pick up the boys. The girls wanted to go, but Vicki wouldn't allow it because that was Antonio's time to spend with his boys. He would pick them up right after school on Friday and he would bring them back to Vicki every Sunday right after church.

It wasn't long before Dr. Collins had finished what the judge ordered him to do.

The judge met with Dr. Collins and Vicki in his office and told Dr. Collins that he was satisfied with the completeness of his work. The judge was working on the schedule for Dr. Collins to pick up his children when Vicki said, "Your honor, I have Beth in pre-school and I would like for Matthew to pick the children up on Friday and bring them back on Sunday afternoon, like Antonio does." Dr. Collins began to smile at her and said, "That would work for me."

The judge said, "So ordered."

Then Vicki said, "I don't want my children going out of the state at any time."

The judge said, "So ordered."

Then Vicki added, "I want Matthew to be the one to keep them and not a servant."

The judge looked at her and he said, "So ordered."

Dr. Collins said, "I don't know how to cook or clean." The judge said, "Well, son, it's time for you to learn."

Dr. Collins said, "Vicki, I was looking at some houses in your neighborhood, not on the same street as you. How would you feel if I moved there?"

"What about the mansion in California?"

"Oh, I'll let the butler stay there. He was there when I was born. He will keep the place up."

"What about the hospital?"

"I can open up a practice here and, every now and then, I will check on all of the hospitals."

The judge said, "It sounds good to me."

So Dr. Collins bought a four-bedroom house with two baths just three streets over from Vicki. All three parents were allowed to see the children all the time. That following Friday, the children arrived from school. The doorbell rang, and it was Antonio coming to pick up Antonio Jr. and Ja'cob. The girls went running to the door with them. They were saying their goodbye's for the weekend.

Antonio spoke to Vicki, but he really didn't have anything to say to her. He would just get his boys and would leave. It wasn't long before Dr. Collins would show up to get his children, Beth, Angel, and little Matthew Jr. Vicki was standing at the door waiting for him. As Dr. Collins was putting the children into the car, he would talk to Vicki about giving him another chance. She said, "Matthew, you are going to have to prove yourself to me before I could ever think of anything like that." After everyone left, Vicki jumped up and down happily because she had the whole house to herself. Vicki began to clean the house and, as she was moving things around, she noticed this picture that had fallen behind a chair. It was a picture of her and Antonio after the graduation party. Vicki remembered when the picture was taken. As she was looking at it, she remembered a little more about that night. She took the picture and ran outside with it. She was going to show Antonio and tell him that she remembered that night. But as she was about to go through the park, she saw Antonio with some woman. As she approached him, Antonio said, "Vicki, may I help you?" She said no.

Antonio said, "Let me introduce you to a dear friend of mine. This is Mary, and Mary, this is Vicki." Mary said hello to Vicki as she held Antonio's hand. Vicki spoke to her and said, "Will you both please excuse me." As Vicki was walking away, she threw the picture down.

When Vicki went back into her house, she went upstairs to call her father. She called and asked him to call his lawyer to file for her divorce. Mr. Smith tried to talk Vicki out of it. Vicki said, "Look outside in the park!!"

When Mr. Smith walked to the window, he could see Antonio kissing Mary. Then he said, "Okay, Vicki, let me call him right now."

Vicki said, "Antonio's life has been on hold too long. He deserves to be happy. I'm looking at them and I can see they seem to be happy with each other and I'm stopping his happiness."

Mr. Smith said, "Well, let me hang up so I can call you a lawyer." "Please tell him to file it right away."

Vicki went back to cleaning up. As she was cleaning, she began to cry. She was feeling jealous of Antonio and Mary. After Vicki finished crying, she took every picture that she had of her and Antonio together along with her letters from him and she packed them away.

After she finished cleaning, Vicki lay down. It wasn't long before Beth and Angel called her crying.

Vicki yelled, "What's wrong!?"

Beth said, "Dad is cooking and he has smoked up the house and the alarm is going off! We are scared, Mom, come and get us."

Vicki jumped up and drove over to Dr. Collins' house. When she ran into the house, smoke was everywhere. She took the girls by their hands and then brought them outside. She told them to sit in her car until she got back, while she saved their dad. The children were so scared. Vicki went back in and began to open up all of the windows. Matthew was running around trying to put the fires out. As he was running from the kitchen, Vicki said, "Matthew, what are you doing?!"

"I was trying to cook for the children but they were fighting and Matthew had left the kitchen. So I left the food for one minute and everything burnt up."

"Did you take everything off the stove and cut everything off?" "Yes."

As she was walking into the kitchen, she just threw the burnt pots into the trash can. Finally, the alarm stopped going off. Vicki sat down and said, "My God, Matthew, what are the children going to eat?"

Dr. Collins said, "Vicki, I have never cooked in my life." "Well, I see it now."

"Let's go outside until this smoke gets out of here."

As Dr. Collins and Vicki were sitting on the porch, Dr. Collins stood up and went to get the children out of the car. They decided that they were neither getting out, nor staying with their dad. Everyone cried, "No Dad, we are going back with Mom!"

Dr. Collins said, "Oh, so no one wants me?" Everyone shook their head no! Vicki began to laugh out loud. Dr. Collins went back to the porch and sat right beside Vicki and began to laugh out. "I think that I have scared our children."

Vicki said, "I think so." As he watched Vicki laughing, he looked into her eyes and said, "What's wrong, Vicki? Why have you been crying?"

"You wouldn't understand." "Try me."

Vicki said, "I saw Antonio kissing and holding hands with some girl named Mary today in the park."

Dr. Collins asked, "How did that make you feel?"

"I got jealous."

He asked, "Do you love him?"

"I really don't feel anything for him, but the idea of holding onto two men is a fantasy of mine. It's many women's dream to control them to where you want them."

He said, "So that's what it is."

They both began to laugh. Then Vicki said, "I told my dad to call his lawyer and file for my divorce." Dr. Collins just looked at her, but he didn't say anything. After they both sat there for about five minutes, Vicki said, "Matthew, lock up your house.

I'm taking you all out to the best pizza place ever." He said, "Who's driving?"

Vicki answered, "Who do you think? I am." As Dr. Collins was getting into the car, one of the girls wanted to know "Where is dada going?" Vicki said, "I'm taking you to eat some pizza." The girls yelled out with laughter.

When they arrived at the pizza parlor, the waitress took their order. Vicki put Matthew Jr. into his baby seat and the girls were having so much fun. Dr. Collins and Vicki were talking and laughing, too, until Antonio Jr. and little Ja'cob walked over to their table. They yelled out, "MOM! What are you all doing here?"

Vicki asked, "Boys, who are you two here with?"

Antonio Jr. said, "We are here with Dad and his friend," as he pointed back to Antonio. Vicki looked at Dr. Collins. Both men saw each other at the same time. Neither one of them spoke to each other. Then Antonio and Mary approached the table to get the boys. Vicki said, "Hello, Antonio." And she said to Mary, "Well, we meet again."

Mary said, "So we do."

Dr. Collins kept looking at Vicki and then he said, "Will you all excuse me for a minute, I really need to wash up for dinner." As he was getting up, he reached over and kissed Vicki and then walked away. Antonio just looked at him.

Vicki looked up at Antonio and Mary and said, "Please don't let me keep you away from your dinner." Then she said, "Boys, give me a kiss and go back to your table to eat. Okay?"

The boys said, "Okay, Mom." As they were walking away, the boys looked back at their mom and their sisters and baby brother and they both said, "We love you, Mom."

Vicki said, "Now you know that I love you." By now, Dr. Collins was walking back to the table.

Antonio said, "Come on boys, let's finish eating."

Vicki looked at Matthew and said, "Thank you."

He said, "No one is going to make a fool out of my Vicki." As everyone was eating, they would check on each other every now and then. All the children were having the best of times, but all the adults had so much tension between them. Finally, Dr. Collins said, "Vicki, the children have finished eating and little Matthew has fallen off to sleep in his plate."

As they were getting ready to go, the boys ran over to their mother to say good-bye. She kissed them and said, "You all have a good time. I will see you both on Sunday."

When they reached the car, the girls said, "Dad, we are going home with Mom."

Dr. Collins said, "Okay, because there may still be smoke in the house." As Vicki was driving, she didn't say anything. The children fell off to sleep. Dr. Collins said, "Vicki, a penny for your thoughts."

"You know, I think that I felt sorry for him. And now I don't. But he can't say anything about you being around the boys when he has Mary around them. What is good for him is also good for me."

Dr. Collins said, "Oh, I feel trouble coming."

She said, "No, I'm not going to challenge her. But he better not say anything when we are together with the boys."

Dr. Collins looked at Vicki and said, "You are not planning on using me are you?"

Vicki looked at him and said, "You are in this thing with me for life."

He looked back at the children and then looked at Vicki. He said, "I have never seen this side of you."

When Vicki arrived home, Dr. Collins helped Vicki take the children to their bedroom and they put them to bed. As they were coming back downstairs, the phone was ringing. It was Vicki's father. Mr. Smith said, "I talked to my lawyer today and he had the paper typed up. The courts are having Saturday court tomorrow and he is taking the paper to the judge in the morning to be signed by him, then the carrier will be taking Antonio his copy. Are you sure that this is what you want?" Vicki said, "Dad, you just make sure that those papers are in Antonio's hands no later than noon tomorrow. Bye, Dad, I love you."

Dr. Collins was standing right beside Vicki. He said,

"Vicki, please put my ring back on. It cost me over two million dollars."

Vicki put the ring back on, then she said, "Matthew, I do love you, but please don't ever hit me or scare me again." Vicki took Dr. Collins upstairs with her. After taking a shower together, Dr. Collins slept with her.

Dr. Collins was so happy that he began to sing a song that Elvis Presley sang. The song was "Bridge Over Troubled Water."

When you are weary, feeling small

When tears are in your eyes, I will dry them all,

I'm on your side, when times get rough

And friends just can't be found

Like a bridge over troubled water

I will lay me down

Like a bridge over troubled water

I will lay me down

When you're down and out

When you're on the street

When evening falls so hard, I will comfort you

I'll take your part, oh, when darkness comes

And pain is all around

Like a bridge over troubled water

I will lay me down

Like a bridge over troubled water

I will lay me down

Sail on silver girl, Sail on by

Your time has come to shine

All your dreams are on their way

See how they shine

When you need a friend

I'm sailing right behind

Like a bridge over troubled water

I will ease your mind

Like a bridge over troubled water

I will ease your mind

After Dr. Collins finish singing, Vicki just laid in his arms and she went off to sleep.

The next morning, Antonio received his divorce papers even sooner than Vicki thought that he would. Antonio left the children and ran through the park to Vicki's house with the paper in his hand. When he knocked, no one answered, so he used his keys to let himself in. When he went upstairs, he saw Dr. Collins and Vicki in bed asleep. He yelled at Vicki, "Vicki!!!! This is what you want?! You got your divorce then, but I'm taking you back to court because this man will never be around my boys."

Vicki said, "Who do you think that you are talking to, Antonio? You had Mary around my boys. I have enough money to keep you in court for a very long time. Get out of here!" They were both so loud that it woke up the children. Before Antonio left, he signed the divorce papers and threw them at Vicki.

Dr. Collins laid back and laughed at him.

Antonio was so mad that he went to Vicki's father and talked to him. Mr. Smith met with him. After they talked, Mr. Smith called Vicki and said, "Is Matthew Collins over there in bed with you?"

"Dad, I love Matthew and I'm going to marry him. Antonio wanted to have his cake and eat it too."

Mr. Smith said, "I don't like this, Vicki."

"Dad, this is my business, and if you or anyone else tries to stop me, I will move away with him and all of my children and no one can stop me." Mr. Smith didn't say anything else.

That evening, Pastor Tucker called Vicki to his office because he just wanted to talk to her. As he finished talking to her, he said, "Vicki, I need you to do something for me. Tomorrow at church, the all-male choir is going to sing and I want you to sing my favorite song with them. I used to love for you to sing. And bring your Dr. Collins."

Vicki said, "Do you want me to practice with them now?"

He said yes, and as they were walking toward the group, Pastor Tucker said, "We can't help who we fall in love with. You do what you think is best."

Vicki began to sing a song written by Reverend Johnnie Holloway and the Gospel Jubilee Singers titled, "Lord, Lift Me Up".

The next morning was Sunday. Vicki got up to go to church, and she asked Matthew to come with her but he said no, so she left the children home with him. She was so nervous about singing in front of everyone. Antonio didn't know that Vicki would be there. He walked into the church with Mary in his arms and he and Vicki's two boys. They went and sat down right beside his parents.

Vicki was looking inside the church and saw her mother and father enter. She was so surprised to see them.

When church started, Pastor Tucker stood up and said, "We have a special treat for everyone." When the all-male choir walked out, Vicki walked out with them to sing the lead part. As she began to sing, the door came open. It was Dr. Collins and their children. As she was singing, Vicki began to cry.

Everyone began to look back and they began to whisper, "Isn't that the billionaire?" Antonio began to cry. Dr. Collins never sat down. He just stood and looked at Vicki while holding onto little Matthew. The girls went to sit down with their brothers. When Vicki finished singing, Dr. Collins cried out, "Vicki, Vicki, I love you!" Mary just held onto Antonio.

Two months later, Antonio and Mary were married and Vicki and Dr. Collins were also married. And they all moved to another town. But not too far from each other, because Antonio and Vicki still shared custody of their children.

THE END